TO WALK IN THE SUN AGAIN

In the 1920s, Victoria, still grieving for her dead husband, goes to work for elderly Edward Mansel. When she meets her employer's grandson, Andrew, who had been injured in the First World War, he makes no secret of the fact that he has fallen in love with her. But Victoria will not allow herself to love Andrew, despite her young son's great affection for him. Was the tragedy of her past always going to get in the way of her future happiness?

Books by Ann Redmayne
in the Linford Romance Library:

A TIME TO FORGET
TO SPEAK OF LOVE

ANN REDMAYNE

TO WALK IN THE SUN AGAIN

Complete and Unabridged

LINFORD
Leicester

First published in Great Britain

First Linford Edition
published 2000

British Library CIP Data

Redmayne, Ann
 To walk in the sun again.—Large print ed.—
 Linford romance library
 1. Love stories
 2. Large type books
 I. Title
 823.9′14 [F]

 ISBN 0–7089–5636–X

Published by
F. A. Thorpe (Publishing) Ltd.
Anstey, Leicestershire

Set by Words & Graphics Ltd.
Anstey, Leicestershire
Printed and bound in Great Britain by
T. J. International Ltd., Padstow, Cornwall

This book is printed on acid-free paper

1

As Victoria walked the short distance from Lemster railway station, she wondered whether avoiding telling Edward Mansel her true circumstances had counted as a lie. Although at her interview she had answered his questions truthfully, she hadn't volunteered anything extra, like, for instance her three-year-old son, Alexander.

Edward Mansel had hardly looked at her, asking her abrupt questions as he read her references. So she was surprised when he wrote to say she should start at once as his secretary. A strict churchgoer, he believed no work should be done on the Sabbath, and so that was to be her day off. Turning from Worcester Road into Pinsley Road, she smiled at the thought that this would enable her to go to Ludlow every week to her mother, who

1

was looking after Alexander.

Pausing at the gate into the Priory churchyard, she looked sadly at the peaceful surroundings. The warming sun of May, 1920, seemed a world away from the cold mud of France where her husband, Philip, had been killed. If only he was buried somewhere she could go to, tend.

But straightening her shoulders, Victoria walked on quickly, turning into Church Street where beautiful houses enjoyed the serenity of their nearness to the Priory at one end, whilst at the other, lanes and narrow roads were lined with small, busy shops. Reaching Upper House, she saw a sack-aproned woman on her knees furiously scrubbing the already immaculate steps. She must be the daily cleaner Mr Mansel had mentioned.

'You'll be that new sectree then,' the cleaner said but neither paused nor looked around. 'I hopes you keep that study of his tidier so I can clean proper like.'

'I'll do my best,' Victoria promised.

Getting stiffly to her feet, the cleaner used the back of her work-reddened hands to push away grey hair.

'My, but you're tall! And you could do with some of Mrs Pritchard's good cooking by the looks of you.'

Embarrassed by this scrutiny, Victoria began to introduce herself.

'Oh, I knows yer name. Heard him telling Mrs Pritchard. Everybody calls me Polly. Now, Mrs 'ampton, you come along with me,' Victoria was told firmly as Polly led the way into the cool, black-and-white hall. 'I'll just tell him yer here,' she said, knocking loudly on the front door on the right. 'You have to knock loud to get his attention he's so wrapped up in his work.'

Barely lifting his head from the book he was reading, Edward Mansel told Victoria she could have until lunch time to unpack the small trunk that had come ahead of her. The bedroom she had been given was on the second floor at the front of the house, with the cook-cum-housekeeper, Mrs Pritchard, having a room at the back.

Propping the faded sepia photograph of Philip on the chest of drawers, Victoria did not put the one of Alexander with it, but slipped it under handkerchiefs in the top drawer. It would never do for Polly to see it and somehow Mr Mansel learn she had a child. He had made it very plain that he demanded undivided loyalty and he might well see Alexander as occupying a corner of Victoria's thoughts that weren't entirely his.

Patting her corn-gold hair coiled back behind her ears, Victoria craned to see her reflection in the tarnished wall mirror. She and her mother had scraped to get the money to buy two straight, knitted skirts and the wool to make three toning jumpers. Previously she had worked part-time in a bookshop where an overall hid the shabbiness of her clothes. But although Mr Mansel hadn't mentioned it, she knew she would have to be presentable as his secretary, for he held a respected position in the writing world. She had also managed to purchase two blouses quite cheaply.

She went downstairs earlier than arranged, eager to show she was not one to loiter. Mr Mansel was paying her far more than she had earned in the bookshop, making all the differences between just about making ends meet and being able to afford better food for Alexander and her mother, as well as occasional treats for the little boy. But just as Victoria was about to knock on the study door, she was astonished to hear Mr Mansel's voice raised in rage.

'Get out of my sight, you ungrateful layabout. I offer you a chance to make something of yourself and you have the temerity to tell me that you belong to no-one. Well, Mr High-and-Mighty, I shall take that to its logical conclusions and alter my will.'

Wildly looking for somewhere to

go, Victoria quickly opened the door opposite which she found led into the dining-room, but she wasn't alone, for, tight-lipped, Mrs Pritchard was laying the table for one.

'I . . . ' Victoria began aware that Mrs Pritchard knew she had overheard. 'I thought I would wait here until Mr Mansel is free.'

The study door slammed and a deep voice muttered angrily, 'I'm not a child to be ordered about.'

Then the stained glass in the front door rattled alarmingly as Mr Mansel's visitor slammed that, too.

'You'd better come along with me to the kitchen and have a cup of tea until he calms down,' Mrs Pritchard said, leading the way. 'He shouldn't go talking like that to Mr Andrew, not in his state of health.'

Victoria waited until they were seated either side of the large kitchen range before she asked hesitantly, 'Who's Mr Andrew?'

'Andrew Mansel, Mr Mansel's only

grandson. And he was so badly injured in France that it's a crying shame to see him. He was so active before, but he and Mr Mansel have never quite seen eye to eye. One's as stubborn as the other. Even before the war, they were arguing something dreadful about what Mr Andrew should do. Mr Mansel wanted him to go in for the law, but Mr Andrew wanted to paint, still does as far as I can gather.'

Seeing that Mrs Pritchard was not averse to gossiping about their employer, Victoria asked what he had against artists.

'He says they're always so poor they can't support a wife, leastways one from a decent family.'

'Surely it's no concern of his, whom his grandson marries?'

'Mr Andrew is his only hope of a great-grandson and Mr Mansel wants the boy to be well connected, to have a mother whose family can open the right doors.'

'Money and position aren't everything,'

7

Victoria said softly, remembering her own love-filled marriage. 'They don't automatically bring happiness.'

Something in her manner made the elderly cook lean forward to pat her hand.

'It's hard, isn't it, when they've gone?'

'You, too?' Victoria asked, with a sad, questioning smile.

'My Fred was killed just before the Boer War ended in 1902. My children are all married now with homes of their own and so it suits me to be here. He's not a bad sort, Mr Mansel,' she finished. 'It's a pity Mr Andrew won't be coming here, for he could do with seeing a young, pretty face.'

But Victoria wasn't at all sorry, for although Philip had been dead for two years, she felt she could never look at another man. As Victoria went into the study, Mr Mansel looked up from his desk, his eyes shrewd, enquiring.

'Just come down, have you?' he said abruptly.

She nodded. What was it about this man that she was yet again concealing something? But what would it achieve if she told him she had heard him threaten his grandson?

'Very well then,' he said, dragging a large, dusty box towards him. 'As you know, my latest book is about this lovely county of ours, Herefordshire. In my younger days, when I was able to walk twenty miles without thinking about it, I filled numerous notebooks with details about the plants, animals and trees and also about the old buildings and long-forgotten paths. I need your help to bring those notes into some sort of order. Now I suggest this way will be best.'

And so for the next hour the two of them worked amicably, looking through the notebooks, trying to find the best place for Victoria to start. She was amazed at finding yet another side to her employer. At her interview he had seemed offhand. With his grandson he was impatient, dictatorial and yet now, immersed in his notes, he was eager, relaxed. But when Mrs Pritchard came in to say lunch would be in ten minutes, Victoria was astonished to find she was to eat by herself in the dining-room, whilst Mr Mansel's meal was brought to him on a tray.

'You needn't have bothered to lay the table for me,' Victoria said as Mrs Pritchard brought in a succulent pork chop and vegetables. 'I could have a tray with Mr Mansel.'

'No, it wouldn't do. Mr Mansel would be uncomfortable. He's not used to people, you see. He could really do with Mr Andrew's company, but then you never know, in time you might do.'

Victoria smiled vaguely. She didn't want any involvement with Mr Mansel other than as his employee. If he wanted company, then let him make it up with his grandson.

Although she soon found her work was interesting and time-consuming, Victoria found the evenings long and

10

lonely. Sensing that Mrs Pritchard did not want her dropping into the kitchen for a chat, she always waited to be invited. Every day, she wrote to Alexander and her mother, sometimes telling them of interesting things she had discovered in the notebooks. These letters were painful to write and several times she would stop to pick up the child's photograph, tears misting her eyes.

She missed Alexander so much, even his naughtiness. Her mother's small home might not be as grand as Upper House, but it was always filled with Alexander's non-stop chatter and laughter.

Despite its comfortable furnishings, Upper House was like a mausoleum. Then Victoria would smile at the chaos Alexander would bring to such a house, and picking up her pen would finish the letter. She knew not to look for replies. Brought up on a remote farm, her mother had little schooling and although she could read, putting pen

11

to paper was beyond her.

On the third evening after posting a letter, Victoria went into the surprisingly large Priory church and, sitting in a quiet corner, let the peace of the centuries-old building flow over her. Her thoughts had drifted off like small clouds on a sweet breeze when a sudden clatter echoed sharply.

'Who's there?' she called, rising and taking a few, uncertain steps.

There was silence followed by very faint sounds as though someone was trying to be very quiet. Without stopping to think a thief might be robbing the poor-box, Victoria ran light-footed towards the noise. Rounding a pillar, she broke into a run when she saw a man struggling to get to his feet.

'Are you all right?' she asked, as he stood up awkwardly.

It was only then she noticed the stick lying under the overturned chair, drawing materials scattered over the stone floor.

'Here,' she said, picking up the stick and holding it out to him.

She had presumed his set face had been caused by the shock of the fall, but there was no excusing the way he almost wrenched the stick from her.

'Of course I'm all right!'

There was something in the tone of his voice that made her frown in half recognition. Where had she heard it before?

'I'm not a child to be . . .'

'Andrew Mansel.'

Although she only whispered the name, he glanced at her sharply.

'I don't think I know you,' he said, looking at her intently.

She was tall but still she had to look up at him, meeting his intense dark eyes with a calmness she was far from feeling. How thin he looked, pale, too, dark shadows under his eyes telling of sleepless nights.

'I work for Mr Mansel.'

'Ah, the sectree,' he said, imitating

Polly, a faint smile indicating humour not malice.

She nodded as they stood awkwardly, neither knowing what to say next and each hoping the other would speak first. Hearing the clock strike nine and knowing Mr Mansel locked the doors about that time, Victoria was precipitated into saying something.

'I know you're not a child, but let me help you pick up your things.'

They both bent down, he awkwardly, stiff-legged, slightly off balance. She was graceful, swift and when she handed him the pad her smile was genuine. But also there was a certain something, a warning that it was not an invitation for further conversation.

Watching her walk away quickly he thought it the sort of smile she would give to anyone she helped, from a doddering, old man, to a child whose ball had rolled away. He wondered if she would turn, perhaps to see if he was all right, but she did not. What, he wondered, had his grandfather told her about him. But what did it matter? Whether she was good at her job or not, his grandfather would soon begin to resent having another person around him all day.

Slinging the canvas bag containing his drawing things over his shoulder, Andrew Mansel walked slowly out of the Priory. He hoped his grandfather wouldn't sack her just yet and when he did, it would be gently done. There had been shadowed pain in her eyes, and something else hinting at emotional imprisonment. And Andrew knew that feeling, only his imprisonment was more physical.

2

Victoria's first weekend back in Ludlow with Alexander was a mixture of happiness and sorrow. It was a joyous reunion, for although her mother wouldn't say so, the child had been pining. This was soon forgotten when Victoria delved into her bag to produce a small parcel.

Alexander tore away the brown paper, delighted to find a tiny, brightly-coloured tin horse, mane and tail flying, saddle red, with yellow stars. For her mother, Victoria had bought a pale-purple bottle of lavender water, the first time Mrs Davy had had any scented preparation.

'I don't know if I should be using such things at my age,' she said, whilst sniffing appreciatively at the dab Victoria put on her wrist. 'What ever will people think?'

'They will hardly think you a fallen woman,' Victoria teased. 'But if it makes you feel easier, just use it in the evening when there's no risk of anybody finding out. Or you could put a few drops in the rinse water of your underwear.'

'Victoria Hampton, what's come over you! I'll do no such thing. You've been away barely a week and already you're full of unseemly thoughts.'

On the Monday morning, with heavy heart, Victoria caught the milk train back to Lemster. Mr Mansel had raised no objections other than to warn that he would expect her to be working promptly at nine. Victoria had not said goodbye to Alexander, slipping away whilst he was still asleep. She hoped her mother was not having to cope with too many tears when the small boy realised she had gone again. But Victoria had promised another surprise for the next Saturday and that might prevent any tears.

She had no need to knock at Upper

House door, for Mrs Pritchard had seen her from the dining-room where she was laying the breakfast table.

By mid-morning, Victoria didn't know if indeed she was being slower than usual, but Mr Mansel seemed to criticise her every few minutes and with mounting irritability.

'I warned you that I did not expect your efficiency to be marred by travelling on such an early train,' he said eventually. 'I shall have to reconsider giving you every Sunday off. Perhaps instead it should be three days, once a month.'

'No!' Victoria said so sharply that Mr Mansel looked at her with a frown of annoyance. 'I'm sorry, it's just that I'm finding the room a little airless. May I open a window?'

'Certainly not! I don't want my papers blown all over the place.'

Victoria smiled inwardly. For a man who, when young, had loved being out in the country, Mr Mansel now showed little inclination for fresh air.

'You can have a break. Take a turn around the garden,' he said.

'Will you come with me?' she asked mischievously, heading to the door.

He shook his head without looking up from his notebook.

Victoria went through the French windows of the drawing-room into the high-walled garden. Surprisingly large for a town house, it was tenderly cultivated by a gardener who came in three days a week. Monday was not one of those days and Polly had hinted darkly that he would be too fuddled from a weekend drinking the local strong cider to be safe wielding a hoe.

Halfway along a path, a green-painted iron seat was framed by an arch of early pink clematis and here Victoria sat, letting the birdsong and rose perfume calm her. It was the back door opening that made her peer from her secret arbour. What Victoria saw made her frown, for Polly was carefully tucking a piece of old tablecloth around the contents of an obviously laden basket. Then Mrs Pritchard came running out with a small apple tart which she quickly tucked under the cover. There was something in their manner that indicated this food wasn't going to any charitable cause sanctioned by Mr Mansel. Surely Polly, with Mrs Pritchard's connivance, wasn't stealing?

Waiting for a few minutes, Victoria returned thoughtfully to the house. What should she do? She knew nothing of Polly's circumstances. Cleaning paid very little and perhaps she had many children to support, aged parents, too. So, reluctant to condemn anyone without finding out all the facts, Victoria decided she would try to find out more about Polly.

That evening, on her way back from posting her daily letter to Ludlow, Victoria turned into a street of small houses she had not seen before. It was a moment or two before she recognised the figure hurrying along in front of her. She thought nothing of this, for cleaners often worked in several houses and offices. But then Polly stopped, knocking urgently at a door which opened. Polly stepped inside quickly. There was no mistaking the cloth-covered basket over her arm. Stopping behind an overhanging lilac bush, Victoria pretended to be searching in her bag.

What should she do? If she walked on past the house, Polly might well see her and think she was being spied on. But the house looked too good for it to be Polly's home. Victoria had half-turned away to retrace her steps when she heard a door open and then close swiftly, followed by hastening footsteps as Polly continued down the narrow street, the basket now swinging empty in her hand.

Puzzled, Victoria turned and walked past the house. Could it be that Polly and Mrs Pritchard were really obeying Mr Mansel's orders, perhaps taking food to an old friend of his? Perhaps

Polly's furtive air was because the recipient did not want the neighbours to see he was accepting charity. She walked past the house, then froze as the door opened.

'Out you go!' a voice came booming out.

The order was followed by a loud protest from a tabby cat no doubt annoyed at being swept up from a comfortable chair.

'Hello, there! Mrs Hampton, isn't it?' she then heard.

Victoria froze. That deep voice . . . She intended to turn slowly as though surprised that anyone should be speaking to her. But guilt made her movements rapid. 'I've just come for a walk,' she explained hurriedly.

He limped towards her, using the white picket fence for support.

'As long as you don't feel you're going over to the enemy, would you like to come in for a few minutes?'

She hesitated. Suppose she saw the basket of food? What should she say?

But then, he didn't know she knew. She smiled at the convoluted stupidity of her thoughts.

'Does that smile mean you accept?' he asked. 'I really do feel I owe you an apology for the other evening in the Priory. I don't know what it is about me, but I can't seem to accept help when I . . .'

Although he didn't finish the sentence she knew he would never use a word indicating his disability, that he was sometimes clumsy and fell over.

'There's nothing to apologise for, and, yes, it would be nice to come in, that is unless you don't mind your neighbours knowing.'

Her glance darted to where slightly disarranged net curtains indicated watchers.

'Good evening, Mrs Evans.' Andrew waved towards one window, then to another he called, 'You're back better today, Mrs Hedges?'

Imagining the annoyance of the watchers at being caught, Andrew and Victoria both managed to hold their laughter until they were inside.

'Don't you mind that they might never speak to you again?' Victoria asked, sinking down into the shabby armchair Andrew had indicated.

'Oh, they'll both find some pretext of speaking to me tomorrow, just to find out what you're doing here, if nothing else.'

Turning a straight-backed chair away from the table, he sat facing her, his right leg extended.

'I suppose they'll want to know what I am.'

She looked down, studying the faded pattern on the red carpet square. She couldn't look at him. She thought it was because she didn't want to make him aware of the awkward way he was sitting, but deep in her heart a voice asked sadly why couldn't the war have dealt with Philip like that, instead of killing him.

'Oh, they know who you are already.' She looked up, frowning.

'Don't forget Lemster is a small place and my grandfather is well known, and Polly is better than the town crier.'

At Polly's name, she glanced around but there was no sign of the basket.

'It's in the kitchen,' he said flatly, as though just realising her presence in his road might not have been accidental. 'Were you following Polly?'

'No!'

'But you knew about the basket?'

She nodded then in a rush told him what she had seen in the garden.

'And you didn't tell Grandfather?'

'Of course not!' she flared. 'It's none of my business.'

She thrust her chin up as though daring him to contradict.

'And what your grandfather arranges for you is nothing to do with me.'

'He hasn't arranged anything.'

To cover her embarrassment, Victoria looked around the untidy, dusty room. The table had the remains of a scrappy meal, pushed to one side to make way for water colours and the sketch of the inside of the Priory. But then his slightly sardonic smile vanished.

'Damn! I never really thought of you when I asked you in. Suppose your visit here gets back to Grandfather? He might well sack you for it.'

'What, for speaking to his grandson?' Victoria said with forced incredulity, but from what little she knew of her employer, that's exactly what he might do.

'If he does, promise you'll come and tell me,' Andrew demanded. 'It will be my fault and I don't want you skulking off.'

'I am not in the habit of skulking off anywhere,' she announced, before marching firmly out of the house and back up the street.

The watchers, now more discreet, saw and noted. She had come with a message from old Mr Mansel but had been sent packing by the look of her!

Victoria didn't see Mrs Pritchard until the next morning when her hostility was immediately noticeable.

Victoria tried all the usual breakfast-time trivial chatter but the replies were short, almost thrown at her.

'Mrs Pritchard, if I've done something to upset you, please tell me,' Victoria asked outright, not wishing for any hostility to build up.

'If you've done anything?' Mrs Pritchard said indignantly. 'I never thought you would be one to go snooping.'

'Ah, you mean Mr Andrew.'

'I mean you following Polly!'

'Would you believe me if I said I hadn't been following Polly? You know I go for a walk most evenings and yesterday I chanced upon the same street that Polly was in. And when Mr Andrew saw me, he asked me in.'

'And by all accounts you came out pretty smartly. Tell you to mind your own business, did he?'

'No, but what I do in my free time is my business,' Victoria said with quiet firmness. 'And what you and Polly do is your business.'

'Yes, it is our business. But I'm going to tell you anyway. Mr Mansel has always resented that even as a child Mr Andrew had a mind of his own. When he heard Mr Andrew had been wounded, I think the old man felt at last Mr Andrew was in no state to go against him. It was a shock to find him even more stubborn than ever. And as for the food . . . '

'I don't want to know,' Victoria said, holding up a silencing hand.

But taking no notice, Mrs Pritchard continued, 'Mr Andrew's mother asked me to keep an eye on him, see he ate properly.'

'Does she live locally?'

'It's her little house Mr Andrew lives in. After his father died in a hunting accident, she moved there. She said there were too many memories in that big place they had over Hereford way. The old man wanted her to live here, but she told him she had no intention of being his housekeeper. He didn't like that, nor when she remarried last year. Old Mr Mansel might seem to live out of this world, but he likes to keep people on a short rein.'

'Including you?' Victoria couldn't resist asking with a smile.

'I might be his cook but I'm not beholden to him, or anyone,' was the firm reply.

'Well, that makes two of us,' Victoria agreed.

During the next couple of weeks Victoria settled into a busy routine, and to her surprise she became more and more involved in Mr Mansel's work. Sensing this, he responded slowly, guardedly, as though wary of her true intentions. Victoria found this strange after Mrs Pritchard's warning that he liked to control everyone, but then she wasn't family, nor a domestic servant. She was in an indeterminate area, like governesses had been before the war, and perhaps this confused him.

She saw nothing of Andrew Mansel, but then she deliberately kept away from the Priory and the street where he lived. She didn't want any involvement in family disagreements, nor did she want to lose her job. Her private life centred around Alexander, the one precious thing she had to remind her of Philip.

3

Victoria couldn't have put a time on when it had happened, but slowly Edward Mansel's attitude towards their work changed. At first he had been absorbed in the notes she had tried to put in date order, ignoring her unless he wanted help. Often she would have liked to question him about the things he had seen, the places he had visited, but Edward seemed to prefer to keep to his side of the invisible wall he had built around himself.

Then one day Victoria glanced through notes of a chance meeting he had had with gipsies, and curiosity popped out a question before she could stop it. For a few seconds he looked at her, then as though a spark had been ignited he began to tell her about how the gipsies went from farm to farm, helping with seasonal work.

Victoria sat entranced as Edward brought the various characters and work to life. It was as though with the telling he was reliving the scene. Then as suddenly as he had started, he stopped, mumbling awkwardly that prattling didn't get work done. For the rest of the day, he seemed embarrassed, awkward, but the next day he asked almost diffidently if she would like to know more about the notes they were working on. And from then on, Edward seemed to thaw little by little in Victoria's presence.

The ever-observant Mrs Pritchard, hearing Edward's voice more often, and not in anger or muttering absentmindedly, was deliberately late with the tray of tea and biscuits she normally took to the study mid-afternoon. She hoped this would bring Victoria into the kitchen so she could question her. Edward Mansel liked his meals and snacks on time and it was not long before Victoria did indeed come to the kitchen.

'Can I help?' she asked, not wanting to ruffle Mrs Pritchard's feathers by asking directly for the tea.

'Sit down a minute,' Mrs Pritchard invited. 'I've made some of his favourite biscuits and they need a minute to cool.'

As she had been sitting most of the day, Victoria leaned against the Welsh dresser, but something about the way Mrs Pritchard glanced at the closed kitchen door alerted her that the warm biscuits might be an excuse.

'Mr Mansel seems to have found his tongue then,' Mrs Pritchard said with a studied casualness that made Victoria smile.

'Yes, and when he does talk, it's as though he comes to life,' she replied, helping herself to one of the biscuits on the cooling-rack.

'He never spoke to her about his work.' Mrs Pritchard's loud sniff clearly showed disapproval. 'She was that hoity-toity. I never knew what he saw in her especially as she was always on to him about money. Mr Mansel might have been well respected but his books didn't begin to make much until just before she died.'

'When did Mrs Mansel die?' Victoria asked, wondering if her death had caused Edward to withdraw even more into his shell. But from what she could glean from Mrs Pritchard's hurriedly whispered information, Edward's widowerhood had been a blessing when it began ten years previously.

'And that's when he seemed to be determined to influence Mr Andrew more than ever. Pity really. If he'd left Mr Andrew alone, he'd have had company, someone young to breathe warmth into old bones. Mind you, you seem to be doing that. There's nothing like a pretty face to cheer up a man.'

'Mr Mansel isn't the sort to notice a woman's looks, and he's too old!'

'I'll grant you he's into his three score years and ten, but there's many an old dog . . .'

'Thank you, Mrs Pritchard,' Victoria

interrupted hurriedly. 'I'll take that tea tray now.'

Any talk, however vague, of relationships, attraction, brought a knot of fear to Victoria's throat. She wanted no involvement with anyone other than Alexander and her mother.

Mrs Pritchard would have been upset had she realised that her lightly spoken comments would have so promptly reversed Mr Mansel's thawing. Although deep down Victoria knew she was acting unreasonably, it was she who re-erected the wall between her and Edward Mansel. He was quick to notice this and although keenly disappointed that her curiosity had been short-lived, he quickly sank back into talking to her only when necessary.

Although it had been Victoria who had retreated from any intimacy with Edward Mansel, she nevertheless felt a strange emptiness. It was nothing like the bottomless pit she had been plunged into by Philip's death, more a feeling of isolation. Of course this disappeared when she was with Alexander in Ludlow, but suddenly the days in Lemster began to have a barren feel about them, as though she was wandering in a wilderness.

Sometimes she was so full of despair that she sought out Mrs Pritchard for a chat and one late afternoon as the housekeeper was putting freshly-baked bread to cool, the conversation turned to Andrew.

'If I hadn't been all behind today I would've had this bread ready before Polly went,' Mrs Pritchard sighed. 'But Mr Mansel was that crotchety this morning, first about his breakfast and then that he hadn't slept a wink all night because his bedclothes had come loose. He stood over me while I remade it. Well, Mr Andrew will just have to go without his warm bread.'

Here, she slid a sly look at Victoria who seeing it, pretended great interest in the two perky china dogs on the mantelpiece.

'He doesn't get many pleasures,

Mr Andrew,' Mrs Pritchard said so dolefully that Victoria had to hide a smile, for she knew full well her sympathy was being played on. 'It comes to something when fresh bread is the only pleasure a young man has to look forward to.'

'Why don't you take it to him?' Victoria suggested, sinking with exaggerated weariness into the fireside rocking chair. 'I'll hold the fort here, though I doubt Mr Mansel will be wanting anything at this time of day.'

'It's me bunions.'

Mrs Pritchard glanced first at her feet and then at Victoria but seeing none of her ploys were working, she sat down. Guilt made Victoria fetch the stool for Mrs Pritchard to rest her feet and then she took the kettle from the hob and brewed some tea.

'You're a good girl,' Mrs Pritchard conceded, finishing her second cup. 'There's not many in your position would turn her hand to helping like you do. You'll be either an only daughter or the eldest of several.'

'Right first time,' Victoria said. 'My mother wanted a large family, but it never happened.'

'Being the only child, or grandchild for that matter, can be a burden.'

'Oh, no!' Victoria replied quickly, without thinking. 'It's me who's the burden.'

'How's that then?'

Mrs Pritchard's question was as swift as a rapier thrust and to give her time to think, Victoria fumbled for her handkerchief and blew her nose.

'I think I'm getting a cold.'

Mrs Pritchard frowned with indecision. Should she suggest a walk in the fresh air with bread for Mr Andrew might do Victoria good, or should she pursue that tantalising hint about being a burden to her mother?

'Mr Andrew is an only one, you know,' Mrs Pritchard said. 'If he weren't, his grandfather might not be on at him so. But thank goodness his mother doesn't pester him. She's let him have Rose Cottage and then she pays me to see to his food.'

'Andrew's mother pays for it?' Victoria repeated.

She just stopped herself asking why this hadn't been mentioned before, then she would have been saved from thinking that food was being spirited away from Upper House. She didn't hear Mrs Pritchard ramble on about how this arrangement had started, for she was startled by the relief flooding over her that Andrew had not been taking his grandfather's food. It had been lurking darkly at the back of her mind that she didn't want Andrew to be guilty of anything dishonourable.

The evening sky seemed to have sagged to just above roof level, the threatening storm making Upper House feel even more closed-in than usual. In the privacy of her room, Victoria lay on her bed in her petticoat, the window wide open. Wiping the dew of perspiration from her forehead, she wondered why it was that summer storms seemed to be more oppressive than winter ones. Perhaps it was that in winter, houses were snug, comforting but even on normal summer days houses could feel confining.

She glanced at the watch, given to her by Philip for her twenty-first birthday, but she didn't see the time. Instead her thoughts drifted back to Philip. It had taken him months to save for the watch, for as a village school master he had earned very little. But they had had sufficient. The school house was rent free and the large garden which Philip loved to tend in the evenings provided plenty of fruit and vegetables.

It was the threatened storm that precipitated Victoria's slide into self pity, something she normally fought against. If only Philip hadn't seen it as his duty to join up as soon as he saw the war was not going to be won quickly. She had begged him not to go but looking at Alexander lying in his arms, he said softly that he owed it to his son as well as his pupils.

Holding her close he had spoken gently as though soothing a child. The war had to be brought to a swift end before more lives were lost, more families tragically broken. He would be back before she could miss him. But he hadn't come back, and oh, how she missed him! Victoria realised she was about to fall into abject misery. She mustn't give in! She mustn't!

Quickly she dressed and, running down the stairs, stopped just long enough to grab a large black umbrella from the stand. She had to get out, away from the stifling house and her dark thoughts. Normally at that time of day, the streets were deserted, but the threatening storm had brought people to stand in doorways and small front gardens. Inevitably there were called comments about the heat, the storm's nearness. Normally Victoria enjoyed the friendliness of Lemster folk but not that evening. She had to be by herself, to try to regain a little easing for her heart.

She supposed it was natural for her to go to the Priory which for hundreds of years had offered shelter to those wanting comfort. Entering the dim building, she took a deep breath. Glancing around, she was surprised not to see or hear anyone else. The silence was so deep that she held her breath. The tense lines of her face softened a little she sat down, eyes closed, intent on loosing herself in the peace of the place.

The Priory might have safeguarded its cool interior from the heavy air, but even its thick walls could do nothing to reduce the first crash of thunder. Startled, Victoria's hand flew to her mouth but it wasn't quick enough to suppress her cry of alarm. The black clouds had enveloped the Priory in such a deep darkness that the lightening was as frightening as the thunder had been. She stood up, arms wrapped tightly about her. No longer was the spacious interior offering refreshing relief. As the elements hurled themselves against the stone and glass, she felt tiny, vulnerable.

'Victoria?'

It was a shout, and not waiting to wonder who it was, she called out, 'Here! I'm here!'

It was the sound of hurrying, irregular footsteps and the tap, tap of a stick that told her it was Andrew.

'Victoria, what on earth are you doing here?' he demanded as he came nearer. 'Why aren't you in Upper House?'

Her reply was cut short by lightening, followed quickly by thunder. Eyes shut, clapping her hands over her ears, she neither saw nor heard Andrew reach her. When he put his arm around her, she tensed as much in fright as shock. She had not allowed any man to put his arm around her since Philip.

Not understanding the underlying reason for her tenseness, Andrew tried to comfort her. His head bent, nearly touching hers, he began to whisper words of comfort but she thrust him away with such violence that he stumbled. Twisting his injured leg awkwardly, he swore, as much in pain as at her violent rebuffal.

Turning, she ran away, the clatter of her shoes not completely obscuring his angry shout of, 'What's the matter with you? What did you think I was going to do to you?'

4

Breathless, Victoria hammered on Upper House front door and when it was opened, she almost fell inside. Shaking back her wet hair from her eyes, she began to apologise to Mrs Pritchard for dripping on the floor.

'Mrs Pritchard has had the good sense to shelter from this downpour,' came Edward Mansel's voice, sounding disapproving.

'I didn't think. I just wanted to get back here.'

Even though she knew her soaked dress and hair must make her look like a stray, she stood tall as she looked at him. But to her surprise it wasn't censure she saw on his face but a look of . . . was it pleasure? Surely it wasn't because she was soaking wet, cold? She shivered and seeing this, Edward hurried towards the kitchen.

'You go and change whilst I see about getting you a hot drink.'

With the storm still raging, Victoria hurriedly scrambled into dry clothes, eager to be by the warming kitchen range, for Edward Mansel did not believe in fires in any other room from mid-May until mid-October. Although Edward had said he was going to see about a hot drink, she hadn't really thought about it until she opened the kitchen door. Every cupboard door open, Edward was looking around in utter bewilderment.

'I can't seem to find anything,' he admitted.

'I'll see to it,' Victoria said with a smile.

She assumed he would go, but instead he stood uncertainly, almost as though he wasn't sure he should be there.

'Shall I bring you some tea?' Victoria asked, fetching the teapot and teacaddy from the Welsh dresser.

'It's very cosy in here,' he replied.

She looked at him half in pity, half in amusement. Poor man, it was his house but he obviously felt ill-at-ease.

'Why don't you sit by the fire whilst the tea is brewing? From the lovely smell this afternoon I think Mrs Pritchard has baked.'

Handing Edward his tea and cutting a slice of sponge, Victoria sat on the other side of the fire. Darting him a quick glance, she thought it strangely sad that she, the employee, was at ease whilst Edward was not.

'It's still pouring down,' she said, thinking that if he spoke he would feel more comfortable.

When he didn't immediately reply she regretted she had stated the obvious. They had never chatted. She had the impression Edward thought it a waste of time. So the sooner she drank her tea . . .

'Did you mean it, about wanting to be back here?'

His question surprised and puzzled her.

'You were so wet. You could have sheltered in a shop doorway.'

'I never thought,' she said, wondering what he was getting at.

'You saw this house as home? I don't mean as your real home, but as a passable substitute?'

She nodded, smiling, as she replied, 'I am here more than in Ludlow.'

'Of course you are,' he said and then, avoiding her direct gaze, he asked, 'You've family there?'

Victoria paused. If he was going to question her, perhaps it hadn't been such a good idea after all to make him tea.

'I was born there and my mother's there.'

'It's very commendable that you go to her every weekend.'

She tensed. He was thinking her a dutiful daughter when in reality she was seeing her son.

'Oh, look,' she enthused, pointing to the window. 'It's stopped raining.'

She was saved from having to

say anything else by Mrs Pritchard's flurried entry through the back door. Pausing only to nod to the housekeeper, Edward fled.

'Well, I never,' Mrs Pritchard said. 'He's never so much as set foot in the kitchen before. You both look to have made yourselves as home.'

'I hope you don't mind. But I was wet . . .'

'Come in here, did he?'

'I didn't drag him, if that's what you mean,' Victoria replied sharply.

Then, wanting to get Mrs Pritchard away from what was obviously an intriguing subject, she asked, 'Did Mr Andrew enjoy your cooking?'

'He wasn't there when I arrived, but I know there's a key hidden under a pot of geraniums and I let myself in.'

Easing off her shoes and leaning to pick up her slippers warming by the fire, Mrs Pritchard continued.

'With him not there, I did a bit of tidying up. He's like all men, never tidy or clean. Mind you I got precious little thanks when he did come in. I know he was drenched to the skin, but he was that mad I half wondered if he'd been here and had another row with Mr Mansel.'

'They certainly don't get on,' Victoria said, hastily going to the door.

She was far too tired to evade possible questioning from the housekeeper. How was it that she seemed to have been drawn into a web of lies, half truths? And what must Andrew think of her running off like that? When she saw him again, she would have to give a convincing explanation that her reactions had been caused by the thunderstorm.

On the following day, Victoria wondered how things could have changed so markedly in so few hours. The day had begun well with Edward Mansel seeming to have mellowed slightly. He had never asked about her personal welfare before, but he had enquired if she was all right after the previous evening's soaking and had she managed to avoid catching a chill?

Her surprise kept her answer brief and with a slight, embarrassed smile, he had quickly turned to work. But very subtly the atmosphere had changed. When he had a need to speak, he looked at her, albeit hesitantly, rather than address his remarks to his lap. Then there had been his surprising suggestion that she might like to finish early as it was market day.

'Although you will be familiar with street markets, I believe ours is very good. Perhaps you would like to take a look at it.'

Victoria was so surprised that she didn't answer immediately and so Edward had stumbled on.

'Perhaps you could look on it as research for our work, getting the feel of the people and the area.'

Even as she accepted, Victoria puzzled over this apparent thawing of Edward's attitude and she smiled inwardly that he should think Lemster people and market so different from Ludlow's that they needed to be studied. But what did it matter what his motives might be? She would use the opportunity to get a small present for Alexander and perhaps she might bump into Andrew and explain away her behaviour in the Priory by saying she was terrified of storms.

The first of her hopes certainly worked out well for she found a tiny stall tucked away in a corner where an old woman was selling various articles made of wood, including a few simple toys. It was a tiny, beautifully-crafted engine and two goods trucks that caught Victoria's eyes. Alexander was train mad and would love them. She asked the price and, pleasantly surprised, she bought it. Even as a child Victoria's friendly smile had made people want to talk to her, and the old country woman was no exception.

'You got a little lad then?' she asked but not waiting for an answer, she continued, 'I'm glad the train has gone to you.'

'But you don't know me,' Victoria puzzled.

'I might not know your name but I reads faces and yours is a kind one, though you've known suffering, but then there's few who haven't these days. But I always say life's like nature. There are bad times and good. It's hard at times to call to mind that the sun is always there, even if he don't show his face all the time.'

Looking down at the toy which she was still holding, she was just going to ask who had made it, when she was startled by Polly's voice in her ear.

'What you got there then?' And peering into Victoria's cupped hand, she exclaimed, 'Why, it's a toy engine.'

Hurriedly thrusting the toy into her bag, Victoria muttered a hasty goodbye before shouldering her way into the crowd. Later, taking out the toy in the cool solitude of her room, she realised bitterly that she had done the wrong thing. She should have told Polly a lie, said the engine was for a nephew, anything to keep Alexander's existence from being guessed at.

Her stomach knotted with anxiety at the thought that Edward Mansel might hear of her purchase, for Polly was an awful gossip. She tried to still her worry by concentrating on the fact that in all probability Edward let Polly's chatter flow over him. Next morning, when Victoria came upon Polly polishing the grandfather clock in the hall, she forced herself to stop as usual to exchange pleasantries. Now she had a lie ready. The toy was for a friend's son, but to her relief Polly was full of her own problems.

'It's me little lad, he's coughing that bad. I've tried everything. I've rubbed his chest with goose grease and made him swallow a dollop of it but nothing seems to be easing him.'

Victoria knew better than to ask if a doctor had been called, for it was only the well-off who could afford doctors fees.

'Who's looking after him?' Victoria asked.

'Me old mum, but she's got terrible rheumatics in her feet.'

'I'm sure Mr Mansel would let you go home if you explained, or I'll tell him if you like.'

Turning back to polish the clock with harsh vigour, Polly said sharply, 'You'll do no such thing. I must get on with me work. The sooner I've done, the sooner I can be away.'

'If there's anything I can do,' Victoria offered, turning towards the study.

'No, I'll manage,' was the slightly breathless reply.

Yes, Victoria thought sadly, like many others Polly was also trying to manage family problems whilst having to earn very necessary money. She half wondered whether to tell Mr Mansel about Polly's child, but decided against it, for she didn't know if letting Polly go early, he might pay her less.

Still anxious about her own problem, Victoria wondered if Edward had heard about the toy and was waiting to pounce on her. When he greeted her as usual and plunged immediately into work, she hadn't realised she had sighed with relief until Edward remarked on it.

'I hope that sigh doesn't indicate boredom,' he snapped, studying her over the top of his glasses.

'Oh, no,' she replied hastily. 'There isn't much difference between a sigh of boredom and one of contentment, is there?'

Edward seemed more than happy with her reply, for he smiled briefly.

Even in the study, Victoria and Edward Mansel heard the commotion in the kitchen. Sighing heavily, Edward was just asking Victoria to see what had happened when Polly burst in, followed by Mrs Pritchard who was trying to calm the panicking cleaner.

'Oh, sir, is it all right if I goes early? Me little lad has took a turn for the worse. He must be bad for Ma to send for me.'

Obviously out of his depth, Edward turned silently to Victoria.

'Is it whooping cough?' she asked going over to Polly and taking her hands in an attempt to steady her.

Polly nodded dumbly, fighting back tears.

'She's already lost one from it,' Mrs Pritchard explained.

Turning to Edward, Victoria stated, 'Shall I send for a doctor?'

'Of course, anything you think will help,' Edward agreed distractedly. 'You go home, Polly. Victoria will see to things.'

Seizing a handful of papers, he bent his head, so removing himself from a disturbing scene. Victoria wasn't the only one to have noticed Edward's use of her Christian name, for after Polly had left and the doctor's visit arranged, Victoria stood in the kitchen waiting whilst Mrs Pritchard made a calming pot of tea.

'I've never heard him call any woman by name before, only that wife of his,' the housekeeper said, looking intently at Victoria.

'Mr Mansel has never done it before. I except it was because he was worried. And you know what he's like when it comes to domestic matters,' Victoria replied defensively.

Although she nodded, Mrs Pritchard was still very curious.

'Perhaps he's seeing you more as family.'

'What a silly thing to say! I've my own family in Ludlow.'

Deciding this line of conversation was heading for dangerous ground, Victoria busily set the tray to take tea and biscuits to the study.

Early that evening, Mrs Pritchard went to Victoria's room, where she was just finishing her daily letter to Alexander and her mother.

'One of Polly's daughters came round earlier to say the doctor's been and with care and good food the little lad will be all right. I've made some chicken soup for him.'

'I'm glad everything's turned out well,' Victoria replied, sliding the letter under the blotting paper pad.

Although the housekeeper's sharp eyes saw this, she was too flustered to remark on it.

'I'm just setting off now with the soup. I've told Mr Mansel. There's some going spare and I thought you might take it to Mr Andrew when you post your letter.'

'I'm sure Mr Mansel wouldn't notice if you were away longer,' Victoria said evenly.

'They live opposite sides of the town, and besides, now Polly isn't here, I've more than enough to do without gallivanting about.'

'All right, I'll take it on the way back from the letterbox,' Victoria agreed, her mind already a maze of thoughts.

What should she say to Andrew? Would he slam the door in her face? Perhaps he would be out and she could leave the soup by the door.

As if Mrs Pritchard had read that last thought she said as she hurried away, 'If he's out, the key is under the geranium pot.'

5

The letter in her pocket, Victoria walked briskly to Rose Cottage. She wanted to get rid of the soup first so she could then enjoy a leisurely walk. She half hoped Andrew would be in the garden so she would be able to lean over the fence and hand over the metal-lidded pot.

But the day had already had so many awkward twists and turns that she wasn't surprised to see she would have to knock at the door. As she waited, her eyes were drawn to the scarlet geranium. She didn't know which would be worse, facing Andrew, or having to retrieve the key and let herself in. So when the front door opened, it was with a wide smile of relief that she thrust the soup at him.

'Mrs Pritchard asked me to bring

you this. She couldn't come. Polly's son is ill.'

'Come in,' he said, making it sound more of an order than an invitation.

'I've a letter to post.'

'Right then, if you want the neighbours to hear, we'll talk here.'

Andrew's tone was hard, his face set, warning that what he had to say was not pleasant.

Ah, well, she thought resignedly, I had better take the bull by the horns.

'About the other night,' she began.

Standing in the tiny hall, the front door shut, she was very conscious of his nearness. She could smell the tweed of his jacket, the soap he used.

'I don't know what my grandfather has been saying to you, but although he thinks artists are decadent, I do not force my attentions on women.'

'I never thought you did. The storm frightened me.'

'I wouldn't have thought anyone with a nervous nature would have lasted two minutes with Grandfather.'

He looked at her steadily and although Victoria tried to match him, a sudden fear made her look away. Since Philip's death she had only been able to look directly at older men, though she couldn't understand why.

'So it is me then,' Andrew said heavily. 'I might have guessed your reaction would be the same. What is it about disability that people shy away from? Dammit, I'm lame, not hideously scarred. People seem to forget why we were wounded. I'm sick of pitying looks.'

'If my Philip had come back, in whatever state, pitying glances would not have mattered one jot. Being alive is what matters.'

Victoria's reply had been quiet and her leaving equally so. Leaning against the wall, Andrew cursed at his crass stupidity. Of course he should have realised she was a war widow. Now it made sense that she flinched, ran away when he had tried to comfort her. She must have been imagining her husband's arms around her.

As she walked to the post box, Victoria wondered why it was that she didn't feel any pleasure in having put Andrew in his place.

One afternoon of the following week, Edward Mansel startled Victoria with an exclamation of delight. Used to him showing little emotion, she looked up to see him reading a letter that had just been delivered.

'Well, this is good news,' he said happily. 'A friend I haven't seen for ages is dropping in to see me tomorrow. Typically he doesn't say what time, but he has business in Hereford. Now does that mean he will be calling on the way there, or on the way back?'

Victoria smiled at Edward's obvious pleasure. Since she had been in Upper House there hadn't been any visitors, which made his estrangement from Andrew even more poignant.

'Does it matter when he comes?' she asked. 'I've plenty I can be going on with. If you will be using the study, I can work in the dining-room.'

'No, I've a better idea. You can have the day off. I'll need all my papers here. There are several things I would like to go over for tomorrow.' Then looking at her over his half-moon glasses, he added, 'You haven't been your usual self these last few days. Fresh air will do you good. Sit in the garden.'

And with that Victoria was dismissed for Edward wanted to sort through his notes ready for his visitor. Going into the kitchen, she braced herself for Mrs Pritchard's outrage that she was expected to prepare a meal for a guest whenever he might arrive.

'It's a good job Polly came back today to get the place clean. And what I may ask does Mr Mansel suggest I serve?'

'He didn't say. You know him. He doesn't really notice what he eats and I expect his friend will be the same. Wouldn't cold meat, pickles and some of your nice crusty bread do? And didn't you say the strawberries were ready in the garden? Add a jug of cream and you've a delicious dessert.'

The housekeeper nodded absently in agreement, her thoughts on something else.

'Did he say who was visiting? I know he writes to a lot of people about his books. If it's someone important, perhaps I should do more than cold meat.'

'From the way Mr Mansel was going through his notes like an excited schoolboy, I guess they'll be spending all the time talking. And you know he doesn't like a fuss.'

Going into the larder to bring out the remains of a leg of lamb, Mrs Pritchard surveyed it thoughtfully.

'I don't know if there'll be enough for the three of you.'

'Don't worry. He's given me the day off. If you don't mind packing me a few sandwiches, I think I'll go for a walk in the country.'

'Fancy him doing that, though I must say since you came he's softened a little. He's paid for the doctor for Polly's lad and insisted she didn't come back until the lad was over the worst. He paid her full wages, and gave her extra for good food for the boy.'

'Just because Mr Mansel buries himself in his work doesn't mean he isn't kind-hearted.'

'You've jumped to his defence quickly,' was the sharp reply. 'His kind heart doesn't stretch to Mr Andrew though, does it? Blood's thicker than water, you know.'

Turning swiftly, Victoria left the room. More than once recently, Mrs Pritchard had commented on the change in Mr Mansel since her arrival. Could it be the housekeeper was jealous? Then as another thought struck her, Victoria drew a steadying breath. Surely Mrs Pritchard didn't think she was setting her cap at Edward Mansel?

Next morning, as she shut the front door behind her, Victoria shifted the wicker basket from one hand to the other. Mrs Pritchard had packed a large picnic for her, even down to a bottle of home-made lemon and barley water. This really was an act of kindness when the housekeeper was obviously busy, but Victoria's thanks had been cut short by the abrupt reply that her money would be better kept for more deserving things than squandering on dubious shop pies. Mrs Pritchard's tone had been such an odd mixture of sharpness and compassion that Victoria once again wondered just how much had been guessed about her family circumstances.

Victoria set off to walk towards Pembridge, a village of half-timbered houses. She doubted she would be able to walk that far, but she always had to have a goal, something to aim for. In the fields on either side of the road, men and women were busy turning the first cut of hay to dry in the summer sun. Pausing on the wide grass verge to watch, Victoria savoured the sweet smell of the cut grass mixing with the creamy elderflowers in the hedges and the last of the wild roses. For the first time since Philip's death she felt a joyousness in being alive. The road behind her was busy with heavy farm carts and so she didn't hear the lighter sound of the pony and trap.

'It's too nice a day to be bad friends, don't you agree?' a voice asked.

A hand over her skipping heart, she knew who it was as she turned to complain, 'You gave me a fright! And what do you mean, bad friends?'

'Do you think you could come a little closer? I don't want our conversation to be heard by half the county,' Andrew said, extending a welcoming hand.

Realising he wouldn't find it easy to get down as good manners would have had him do, Victoria took a few steps closer, but not within reach of his outstretched hand. She stood looking up at him, waiting for him to answer her question. Dropping his hand, Andrew's smile was contrite.

'I want to apologise for the other

evening. I shouldn't . . . '

Not wanting to spoil the lovely day or run the risk of the conversation turning to personal matters, Victoria's smile was more than Andrew had hoped for.

'It's forgotten,' she said firmly.

'Good! But how come you're out here?'

'Mr Mansel has given me the day off. He's having a visitor.'

'Can I make a blanket apology for the rest of the day, for knowing me I'm sure to put my foot in it several times again.'

Shifting her basket from one hand to the other, she put her head on one side as she said, 'You might be planning staying here, talking all day, but I'm not.'

'That's just what I hoped you'd say. So if you hand me the excellent picnic Mrs Pritchard has no doubt prepared for you, let's be going.'

Tightening her grip on the basket's handle, Victoria replied pertly, 'I wasn't aware we were going anywhere.'

'Look, Victoria, I'm going sketching and you can see far more from up here than on foot. And as we're hardly likely to see anyone we know tongues won't be set wagging. Bowling along in this trap is far less exhausting than walking.'

Impatient to be away, the little brown mare pawed the ground.

'It's the pony I'm thinking of,' Victoria said, handing her basket to Andrew. 'She's eager to be off.'

If she had been honest, Victoria would have added that she, too, was eager to be feeling the warm breeze in her face whilst seeing more of the lovely Herefordshire countryside. But her mind was firmly closed to the fact that many girls would have willingly swapped places with her.

It was obvious that Andrew came frequently to Pembridge, for asking Victoria to open a five-barred gate, he turned into the field. Getting down awkwardly, he took the pony out of the shaft to run free and graze.

'Are the pony and trap yours?' Victoria asked, as they prepared to walk the last few yards into the village.

Andrew shook his head as he explained that he sometimes hired them from a shopkeeper in Lemster whose brother owned the field where the pony was now grazing.

'I'm used as a messenger, taking butter and cheese back with me for the shop.' Then more sombrely he added, 'It's good to feel I can be of some help still.'

But then hitching his rucksack of sketching materials on to his back, Andrew picked up his stick and waving it about, said firmly, 'But today's far too lovely to be soured by doom and gloom. Might I suggest you explore the village whilst I sketch? Shall we meet at The New Inn at one o'clock? You can't miss it. It's the very large black-and-white building at the cross-roads in the centre of the village.'

Victoria was happy to agree, for the ride to Pembridge had been mostly in silence, Andrew busy controlling the pony, whilst she enjoyed the countryside. The lack of conversation had allowed her cares and worries to recede and being by herself would be like a healing balm.

So for a couple of hours, she walked slowly, sometimes having to squash herself against walls as a heavy cart trundled past. Finding a path down to the shallow river, she threaded her way through lush grass and flowers to the bank. Secluded, she slipped off her shoes and stockings and sitting down, cautiously put her feet in the surprisingly cold water.

Her thoughts went back to when as a child she had been taken to her grandparents' small farm where she had spent happy hours playing in the stream. If only her grandparents were still alive, she could have taken Alexander to visit there, letting him enjoy running wild. She was oblivious to time passing. But she was not oblivious to the fact that her thoughts were not as despairing as had become normal after Philip's death.

They were more like looking at something she knew she couldn't have, but a substitute would have to do. She owed it to Alexander to give him a happy, secure life so although he would miss not having a father, the loss wouldn't have an adverse affect. Thank goodness she had Philip's son . . .

But then her solitude was shattered by Andrew's shout.

'Do you know what time it is?' he shouted when he saw her. 'I've been worried sick about you.'

She looked up, ready to reply that she wasn't his to worry about, but seeing his red, sweat-dewed face and the clumsy, uneven way he was moving, she felt immediate remorse.

'I'm sorry,' she said. 'It was so pleasant here. I was day dreaming.'

Her face was still soft with happiness and seeing this Andrew felt a strange sense of loss, of being alone. No doubt she had been thinking of her dead husband who was but a grey shadow to him. He looked away, jealous that she had never looked like that whilst with him. But why should she? They were mere acquaintances.

'What was his name?'

The question was out before he could stop it and he tensed, ready for her anger.

'Philip,' she said, as softly and sweetly as a caress.

Then shaking her head as though banishing the thoughts that were no-one's concern but hers, she picked up her stockings.

'Will you keep guard for me whilst I put these on?' she asked, her voice normal, manner brisk. 'I wouldn't want to shock a passerby.'

Reluctantly he turned away. Philip might now be dead, but he had been a very lucky man to have been able to call Victoria his wife.

'Is it too late to go to The New Inn?' she asked, brushing away a stray tendril of hair as she came up to him.

Although he tried to mask his thoughts, his longing to be able to brush that tendril away, she saw and understood.

'Andrew, you asked earlier if we could be friends and I didn't reply because I thought it was the sort of thing said after an unpleasantness. But I'll answer you now. I'm quite happy for us to be friends, but only that. And it has nothing at all to do with your disabilities.'

They looked at each other for a long moment, he with pain that her reassurance might be untrue, spoken out of kindness. But her gaze was steady, open, with no hint of pity or revulsion.

'Then we will be just friends,' he agreed and turning he led the way back along the river bank.

6

Victoria walked slowly towards Upper House still marvelling at the strange contentment which had enfolded her during the day. Andrew had been good company. She was smiling happily when she saw Mrs Pritchard, but one look at the housekeeper's grim face dispelled it.

'Mr Mansel wants you in his study as soon as you come in.'

As Mrs Pritchard took the empty picnic basket, Victoria hastened to obey. What on earth could have gone so wrong? Had she made some awful mistake in her work which Edward Mansel hadn't noticed but the sharp-eyed visitor had? Opening the door, she had barely set foot in the study when, rising from his desk, Mr Mansel accused her of being a liar.

'A liar?' Victoria repeated, dazed.

She had never seen Edward in such a cold, condemning mood.

'Yes, a liar. I had a most interesting visitor today, Howard Reece, for whom you worked in Ludlow. He told me a great deal about you. Obviously you kept nothing from him.'

Victoria closed her eyes to shut out the scene, wishing she was anywhere other than in this angry man's study.

'Lost for words are you, just like you were when I interviewed you? You never told me you had a son.'

Straightening her shoulders, Victoria faced her accuser.

'Not mentioning Alexander was hardly a lie. You didn't ask if I had children.'

'And if I had, would you have denied his existence?'

'No, but then you wouldn't have given me the job, would you?'

'A typical female response! Shifting all the blame on to someone else.'

Victoria bit back her sharp retort to this outrageous generalisation. She had to pacify Edward at all costs.

'Howard Reece knew my circumstances before I worked for him. He lived nearby so knew about Alexander. I'm sorry you didn't know about my son, but I don't see how his existence affects my work.'

'It makes you unreliable.'

'Unreliable?' she echoed in disbelief. 'You haven't complained so far.'

'Women are so bound up with children that if they sneeze once it becomes a disaster and they can't think straight. Look how the cleaning woman had to run off home.'

'Polly didn't run off home. You agreed she could go. If my son is ill, my mother is more than capable of looking after him.'

Pointing to the door, Edward said coldly, 'Mrs Hampton, in the circumstances I shall no longer need your services. I would be obliged if you pack quickly and leave tonight. I shall pay you until the end of the week.'

'You're being totally unreasonable,' she flared. 'But then totally is a word that fits you well. You like total control of people don't you? Andrew . . . '

'So it's Andrew, is it? That's something else you've kept from me. I might have guessed he would set out to get you on his side.'

'It's no good talking to you. I pity you, for you're a miserable, lonely old man and what's more, you enjoy it.'

Less than thirty minutes later, Victoria was half running, half walking to the station. Tight lipped with anger, she was oblivious to the curious glances of passersby. Her haste was more symbolic than necessary for the train wasn't due for another fifteen minutes.

When she heard the steam engine's whistle at Dinmore Tunnel, she waited impatiently at the platform's edge. Usually she looked for a Ladies Only compartment but her thoughts were so filled by the injustice of her dismissal, when the train drew in, she got into the empty compartment in front of her. Out of the corner of her eye she saw the guard go down the train checking the doors but just as the engine was beginning to slowly draw away, her door was flung open and a man fell in, almost at her feet.

'Andrew! Are you hurt?' she asked anxiously as she helped him on to the opposite seat.

Breathlessly he shook his head.

'What on earth made you do such a stupid thing? You could have fallen between the train and the platform and been killed.'

'I wanted to catch you. Mrs Pritchard sent a lad with a garbled tale that you had been sacked and were leaving immediately. That miserable, old man has got it in for me so much that I thought it might be because he had found out about our spending the day together.'

Leaning her head against the high back, Victoria smiled wryly.

'No, it wasn't you. He found out something about me from the friend who called earlier.'

'What on earth has your son to do

with it?' Andrew asked heatedly.

'You know about Alexander?'

'I guessed. I told you Polly was good as the town crier and she told me she'd seen you buy a wooden train. Knowing you go back to Ludlow every weekend, I put two and two together.'

'Mr Mansel says I lied to him, but in my own defence, he didn't ask about my family. Although I was only an employee, he seems to have wanted to control me completely, like he does you. With you it's your career, with me, it's feeling he hadn't got my total commitment.'

'I can afford to tell him to go to blazes, but how will you manage now? I know the war widows' pension is just a pittance.'

'As Howard Reece inadvertently lost me my job, perhaps he'll feel guilty enough to employ me again.'

She closed her eyes and, taking this as a sign that she didn't want to discuss the matter any more, Andrew, too, was silent. But he would have been surprised if he could have read her thoughts, for they were about him. How kind he had been to hurry after her and what it must have cost him in physical pain to do so. Andrew and his grandfather were such opposites, it wasn't surprising they didn't get on.

'Tell me about Alexander,' Andrew asked. 'Is he like you or Philip?'

When she opened her eyes, he saw they were shining with love.

'I suppose he's like both of us. Sometimes a facial expression will remind me of Philip, but my mother says he's very like me at that age.'

As the train wound its way through the lush countryside, Victoria told Andrew about her son and family. He listened with a half smile of encouragement but inside he was seething with anger about his grandfather. As they both got out of the train at Ludlow, Andrew went to look at the timetable for the return train. His limp was more pronounced and he was leaning heavily on his stick.

Victoria was shocked to see how tired he looked, gaunt even. He needn't have come after her.

'Do you have to go back immediately?' she asked suddenly. 'My mother only lives a short walk from here and about now, Alexander will be going to bed and then Mother will be making an early supper. Do come, my mother's cooking is even better than Mrs Pritchard's.'

'I'd like that, if you're sure she won't mind me turning up unexpectedly, especially in the circumstances.'

'You'll be doing me a favour. With you there, she won't go on and on about Mr Mansel. She knows you can't be blamed for your grandfather's behaviour. Come on, we had better get going if I'm to see Alexander before he goes to bed.'

Mrs Davey's neat house was in the middle of a terrace and just a little bigger than Andrew's. But there was no gardens between the houses and the pavement. The front door was ajar in an attempt to cool the house and as Victoria pushed it wide, she called out to her son and mother.

'Whatever are you doing home?' Mrs Davey demanded, hurrying from the kitchen.

Victoria didn't reply for Alexander hurled himself at her, and bending down she scooped him up to hug him fiercely.

'I'll tell you when Alexander's in bed,' she replied. 'Will supper stretch to another one besides me? Andrew was waiting for the Lemster train but there wasn't another due for some time.'

Peering around Victoria and Alexander, Mrs Davey's motherly instinct was aroused by Andrew's obvious tiredness.

'Victoria, don't stand there blocking the doorway. Come in,' she beckoned Andrew. 'I'll make you both a cup of a tea to tide you over until this young rascal goes to bed.'

As Andrew limped in, Alexander looked at him uncertainly, his head nestling into his mother's shoulder for reassurance.

'If only I had my sketch pad,' Andrew muttered, sinking gratefully into a chair in the living-room.

Seeing his admiration, Victoria felt awkward, embarrassed and to cover this, she made much of setting the boy down on the floor, complaining that he weighed a ton.

'Alexander,' Mrs Davey called from the kitchen, 'come and finish your cocoa.'

'Go on,' Victoria encouraged. 'And if you're a good boy I'll tell you a bedtime story.'

Then, turning to Andrew, she warned with a laugh, 'I'll try to be as quick as I can, for Mother will use the opportunity to find out all about you. But if you could entertain Alexander for a minute or two, I'll just tell her briefly about Mr Mansel. I didn't want to say anything in front of Alexander. And also I don't want you to have the awkward job of telling Mother.'

Although Andrew nodded, he wondered whether the small boy would stay with him, but Alexander was a friendly child. Going up to Andrew, his mouth ringed with cocoa, he smiled as he asked, 'Does your leg hurt? Gran made my knee better when I fell out of a tree.'

'I used to like climbing trees, pretending I was in the rigging of a ship.'

'What's rigging?' Alexander asked.

Leaving Andrew to explain, Victoria slipped into the kitchen to quickly explain things to her mother. What she didn't say was that Andrew had come after her. The last thing she wanted was for her mother to get the wrong idea, to matchmake. Not giving her mother time to do more than make angry comments, Victoria went back into the living-room, intending to take her son up to bed but to her surprise he was sitting happily on Andrew's lap. Tears springing to her eyes, she ached with sadness. If only the man holding

Alexander had been Philip! But almost at once she felt ashamed. It wasn't Andrew's fault he had come back from the war and Philip had not.

'Come on, young man,' she ordered, blinking away the tears as she held out her hand. 'Time for bed.' Then seeing his mutinous frown, she added firmly, 'Right now!'

'I want Andrew to take me. He's telling me all about big ships. They're much bigger than houses,' he said, throwing his arms wide.

'No, Alexander, you're coming with me! Andrew is tired.'

'Please,' the boy pleaded, turning to Andrew. 'You can sit on my bed like Mummy does.'

'Well, if it's all right with Mummy.'

Andrew looked questioningly at Victoria and seeing her nod, he put the child down before getting slowly to his feet.

Much to Victoria's surprise, Alexander went to sleep quickly, something he didn't normally do when she came home. Her mother wasn't slow to notice this and congratulated Andrew on his ability to get the child to settle. Curious about how Victoria came to know him, Andrew left it to her to fend off her mother's questions. But after he had finished supper and limped off for the train, Mrs Davey lost no time in questioning Victoria sharply.

'What are you hiding from me?' she demanded, sitting forward in her chair. 'That's a very nice young man. Now, tell me, what's going on between the two of you?'

'Nothing,' Victoria denied, standing in front of the mirror over the mantelpiece, to check her hair unnecessarily. 'I told you, we met in Lemster.'

'You're not the type of girl to be picked up on a street corner and he's not the type to be doing it either. So where did you meet? I'm beginning to think there's something you're ashamed of. He's not married, is he?'

'Of course not. But if he was, I

don't see why that should prevent me offering hospitality to him, considering his health and how tired he was.'

But Mrs Davey wasn't to be deflected. With suddenly narrowed eyes she asked, 'What did you say his surname was?'

'Mansel,' Victoria replied wearily as she waited for her mother's outburst.

'Mansel? So he's something to do with that mean, old devil you've been working for. And where exactly does Andrew fit into the picture? Did the old man disapprove of the two of you? If he did, he's got a cheek for although I say it as shouldn't, you'd be a fine catch for anyone.'

'Mother, there's nothing like that and you forget, I'm not a young girl looking for a husband.'

'Don't talk daft. Of course you're young and although I know you're still grieving over Philip, he'd be the last one to deny you any happiness with another.'

Hands clenched, white-lipped with anger, Victoria stood up.

'Philip is the only man I'll ever love. To even talk about me marrying someone else is to desecrate his memory, our love.'

As Victoria left the room she just managed to suppress the urge to slam the door behind her. To have done so would have woken Alexander, and she did not want him adding to her torment by asking where Andrew was.

'I'll never forget you,' she promised Philip's photograph that night, 'and I'll never let Alexander forget you either.'

7

It was two days later that Andrew was again on a train to Ludlow. Although the previous day he had tackled his grandfather about Victoria's dismissal, Andrew's anger had been so great afterwards that he thought it advisable not to see Victoria until he had regained his composure. He had briefly thought of writing to her but that would have been impersonal, shirking a very unpleasant task.

It was Mrs Davey who opened the door to their unexpected visitor and she was so delighted at seeing him that she nearly pulled him inside. At the sound of voices, Alexander came running and seeing Andrew he began chattering excitedly.

'Victoria's out,' Mrs Davey explained, having settled Andrew comfortably in the living-room.

She didn't say that her daughter had gone to see Howard Reece in the hope of either regaining her old job or getting his help in finding another. Whilst Mrs Davey made the inevitable pot of tea, Andrew dived into his rucksack and brought out a pad of paper and a few crayons for Alexander. Without any hesitation, the small boy climbed on to Andrew's lap and soon the two of them were busy drawing. Coming in from the kitchen, and seeing this, Mrs Davey gasped in astonishment.

'Why I've never seen the boy take to someone so quickly.'

Then, fearful that Andrew might be put off by her comment, feeling he was being trapped in some way, she hurried on, 'But his father was a friendly soul.'

Immediately regretting mentioning Victoria's husband, she banged down the tin tray of the tea things with such vigour that milk slopped out of the jug. Hurrying into the kitchen to fetch a cloth, Mrs Davey muttered apologies about her clumsiness.

Would it always be like this, Andrew wondered, with the mention of Philip, however indirectly, causing uncomfortable moments. If he was to see more of Victoria and her family then that problem would have to be resolved for everyone's sake. But Andrew himself didn't know how to react to his own thoughts about Philip. There were times when he felt jealous of the man although it was he who was dead and not Andrew. Victoria had loved Philip and obviously still did. Could there be room in any woman's heart for two men? And if so, would Philip always have the largest part?

When Victoria came home ten minutes later, she immediately sensed the slight tension, and frowning, she hoped it wasn't because her mother had been tactless in some way. This was reinforced when Mrs Davey hastily got up and, dragging a very reluctant Alexander behind her, went into the kitchen. But however guilty Mrs Davey might have felt, she left the door slightly ajar, the better to hear what was going on.

'Have you been here long?' Victoria asked, firmly closing the door.

Then turning to look directly at Andrew for the first time, she saw the stark greyness of his face, eyes dulled by lack of sleep.

'What's wrong?' she asked, hiding her concern by picking up scattered drawing paper.

Had that dreadful old man made up some tale about her that had brought Andrew to accuse her of some crime?

'Victoria, I really am sorry, but nothing I could say would make him change his mind. But then you know he doesn't listen to me anyway. Perhaps I would have done better to have stayed away, then in a week or so he might have had second thoughts about you.'

'It was kind of you to try, but you mustn't reproach yourself. You know your grandfather — once he's made up his mind about something, he can't be persuaded. In some way I feel very sorry for Mr Mansel. He's such a lonely old man.'

'He's brought it on himself,' Andrew bridled, feeling Victoria was indirectly accusing him of not understanding his grandfather. 'He's always been awkward. From what I can gather he treated my grandmother like a piece of furniture and as for my parents . . . '

'I wasn't implying the family was to blame,' Victoria interrupted. 'It's just that with so many families broken up by the war . . . '

She stopped suddenly, not wanting to say more in case she made matters worse. Andrew had enough problems of his own without making him feel conscious of her widowhood. The silence between them lasted only a few seconds, for, both anxious to break it, they spoke at once. But it was Victoria who continued by thanking Andrew for Alexander's drawing things.

When Andrew left some time later, Mrs Davey turned to her daughter.

'You couldn't wait to get rid of him,' Mrs Davey accused as Victoria leaned thankfully against the closed front door.

'Hush, Mother, he'll hear you! You know how slowly he walks.'

'I've never been so ashamed. I've never made anyone feel so unwelcome in this house that they can't wait to get out of it. That young man had no need to try to get you your job back or to come all this way to tell you.'

Pushing herself away from the door, Victoria frowned.

'I know, I know, but it's more awkward than you think.'

'In what way?' Mrs Davey demanded, following Victoria into the small kitchen. 'What is it you haven't told me? Look at me, Victoria,' she ordered.

'There hasn't been anything going on between the two of you, has there?'

Victoria met her mother's searching look evenly, as with a slight smile she shook her head. Victoria had half a mind to ask exactly what she was accused of, but instead she tried to change the subject.

'As Mr Reece couldn't offer me my old job back, I think I'll call into a few shops and see if there's anything going for me there.'

'There'd be no need for all of this if you'd played your cards right with Andrew. He obviously cares for you. Alexander likes him and so do I.'

'What about me?' Victoria said coldly. 'Don't I count for anything?'

'Of course you do. But from where I am, I can't see anything wrong with that young man.'

'There is nothing wrong with him except I don't love him. How many times must I tell you that I'll always love Philip? He doesn't deserve to be forgotten so quickly. The politician's talk about men giving their lives for their country, but the last time he was on leave, Philip told me that every time he fired his rifle he was doing it for me and Alexander. He didn't want to kill anyone, but he did it for me.'

'Don't talk so daft,' Mrs Davey blustered, though she had been deeply moved by what Victoria had said. 'Like all the rest, Philip had to go. The government saw to that.'

Victoria nodded as she added quietly, 'Yes, but it's what was in his heart that matters to me. I'll never, ever be unfaithful to him.'

Although Victoria visited every shop and office in Ludlow there was no work for her. A few knew she was a widow with a son, but if there was any work available they felt duty bound to give it to ex-soldiers, especially if they were disabled. So without her wage, there had to be severe economies but she and her mother saw to it that Alexander was always fed nutritiously whilst they often filled up with bread and dripping or soup made from vegetables shops discarded, or sold very cheaply at the day's end.

One evening, Victoria was just hurrying back from shopping, when, turning into her street, she bumped into someone. Her apology was abrupt for her thoughts were on Alexander who had that day gone down with measles. More than ever now he would need good food.

'Victoria, what's the matter?'

Shaking her head slightly to come back to the here and now, she looked up into Andrew's anxious face.

'Alexander's got measles,' she said flatly, her eyes showing anxiety.

'Give me your shopping bag,' Andrew ordered. 'I'll carry it for you.'

She began to protest but, taking the bag, he limped off and she had no option but to follow. Arriving at the house, Victoria was just opening the door, when her mother called out, asking what she had managed to get.

'Andrew's here,' Victoria replied, her voice tight.

Taking the shopping bag from him, she risked a glance at him and was relieved that his expression showed concern, but not shock. As he asked her mother about Alexander, she was

100

thankful his thoughts had been on the boy to the exclusion of all else, how much of a struggle they were having to make ends meet.

'Can I see him?'

Andrew glanced at both women, for he wasn't sure whom to ask.

'I've just got him to sleep,' Mrs Davey said, but seeing him half turn as though to leave, she added, 'But come in and have a cup of tea with us.'

Victoria's heart sank. This was the last thing she wanted, for her mother's tongue had a way of running away with her and she didn't want Andrew to know of their near poverty. But for once, Victoria was thankful for her mother's curiosity about Andrew and he didn't seem to mind her questions about his family and work. She was thankful, too, that he didn't stay long, saying he had a train to catch.

He left after asking if he could keep in touch about Alexander's illness and, eager to see him go, Victoria nodded. He was being polite, no more than that, but then as often happened, her mother shattered her thoughts.

'Did you notice how Andrew wouldn't say what had brought him to Ludlow? Every time I asked he side-stepped. Now that makes me think.'

'That makes me think,' Victoria cut in, 'that he thought it none of our business.'

Measles could kill and, very aware of this, Victoria rarely left Alexander's beside. She grew hollow-eyed from lack of sleep and worry. Now it was left to Mrs Davey to scour shops and market stalls for cheap food and, unknown to Victoria, she pawned the few things that might bring a little more money. Looking again into her worn purse in case by some miracle an extra coin had appeared, Mrs Davey was just going out when a railway porter came hurrying up the street.

'I shouldn't be here but I thought you would be needing this in a hurry like. Came in a few minutes ago on the Lemster train.'

As the porter thrust a stout box into her arms, then hurried away, Mrs Davey cried out in delight.

'Victoria, look what we got. It must be food for the box is marked 'Perishables'.'

Hurrying down the stairs to join her mother in the kitchen, Victoria searched frantically for a knife to cut the stout cord. Excitedly, they both delved into the straw packing, exclaiming with joy as they pulled out one delicacy after another.

'Andrew couldn't have done all this, could he?' Mrs Davey said.

Carefully bringing out an apple pie, Victoria said, 'I'd know that beautiful pastry anywhere. Mrs Pritchard has sent this.'

'So does that mean the old misery feels guilty about dismissing you?' her mother asked hopefully, putting a chicken into the zinc-meshed meat safe.

Thoughtfully, Victoria shook her head.

'No, Mr Mansel would never think of such a thing.'

'From what you've said, he wouldn't miss any of this,' Mrs Mansel sniffed.

Victoria didn't contradict her but she knew the housekeeper wouldn't take food without Edward Mansel knowing. No, Andrew was behind this generous and very welcome gift, but she wasn't going to tell her mother that.

Although Alexander's physical recovery was slow, he was soon bored with bed or resting on the couch downstairs. Victoria and her mother played games, told him stories and helped him to draw on the paper Andrew had given him. Occasionally he asked for Andrew and when he did so, his grandmother suggested that he drew a picture for him.

Clutching a few of these, Mrs Davey couldn't look Victoria in the eye as she asked her to send them to Andrew. Predictably Alexander promptly demanded that his mother find an envelope. Victoria refused.

Then, seeing his face pucker ready for an irritable cry, she said hastily, 'But I'll keep them safe and the next time I go into Lemster, I'll put them through his letterbox.'

'We could spare the price of a stamp,' her mother said.

'No,' Victoria said adamantly. 'I've said I'll deliver the pictures when I next go into Lemster.'

'So are you thinking of calling to see if Mr Mansel will take you back again? Or are you too proud? Are you waiting for him to do the asking?'

'I would crawl there if I thought I could get work, but Edward Mansel is as stubborn as a mule. If he could treat his only grandson like he does, then he's hardly likely to soften for me.'

'You never know,' her mother said. 'A pretty face can work wonders.'

Victoria's only answer was a cold look as she left the room. She was annoyed with her mother for suggesting such a thing but she was also acutely aware of her conscience which was constantly reminding her that she hadn't written to thank Mrs Pritchard or Andrew for the food. To write to either of them might be to draw herself into something she wanted to avoid, contact with Andrew.

Alexander's recovery was steady but slow. Victoria and her mother played and read to him but with the irritability of a bored child he was never satisfied for long. Coming in from pegging out a washing, Victoria had suggested her mother go out for a while for a walk or to see a friend.

'It's at times like this I realise I'm not as young as I used to be,' Mrs Davey muttered sadly. 'You were just as trying when you got measles but I coped better.' Then looking at Victoria she added wearily, 'You need a change, too. When I come back, you must have a rest.'

'We'll see,' Victoria said hurrying her mother from the house as Alexander once again began a fretful wail.

'I'm coming,' she said, sharpness edging her voice.

If only Alexander was less of a handful she would be able to look for work again. When, a long wearying half hour later, there was a sharp rat-a-tat at the front door, Victoria assumed her mother had forgotten her key. But it wasn't Mrs Davey but Andrew who was standing there. For a second they stood in silence, both frantically wondering what to say. Then they both spoke together.

Their simultaneous, 'I'm sorry,' made them smile but it was Andrew who continued with, 'Can I come in? This rucksack is rather heavy.'

It was then Victoria noticed that he was leaning heavily on his stick.

'I'm afraid Alexander's in the living-room and in rather a bad temper,' she apologised, standing to one side.

'Good, for he's the one I've come to see.'

Indicating that Andrew should go

ahead, Victoria turned, frowning, to close the front door. Why on earth was she feeling despondent just because Andrew had come to see Alexander? And realising that within minutes Andrew had turned Alexander's fretfulness into smiles, she was even more puzzled by her feeling of depression. Why wasn't she feeling relieved that someone was taking some of the strain of looking after the boy, even though it would only be for a short time?

When Mrs Davey returned and saw Andrew and Alexander engrossed in a story, she did nothing to calm Victoria's unease.

'Now doesn't that do you good to see Alexander happy?' she whispered to Victoria as she turned back into the kitchen where the table was covered with the contents of Andrew's rucksack. 'He must think a lot of Alexander to have carried all of this food. It must have been quite a weight.'

Victoria said nothing, but her thoughts

were heavy as she considered that somehow she was getting trapped by an obligation she would have backed away from, had it not been for the welfare of her son.

8

Victoria knew she would have to thank Andrew for the food but because she hadn't yet done so even for the first occasion, she didn't know how to begin. It was her mother who precipitated things when busy pouring tea. Mrs Davey said Edward Mansel must be a very considerate man to think of sending them provisions. She missed Andrew's surprised look, his frowning glance at Victoria. All she could do was shrug slightly and smile. It wasn't until later she had the chance to explain, and it was her mother who saw that she was alone with Andrew.

When it came time for Andrew to leave, Mrs Davey turned to him and as though Victoria wasn't there said, 'Victoria hasn't been out for days. Fresh air would do her good. So shall she walk to the station with you?'

Andrew's reply of agreement was both instant and enthusiastic for he had been trying to think how he could snatch a few minutes alone with Victoria.

As the two of them walked in silence along the narrow pavement, Andrew was glad his lameness meant their pace was slow. He wanted to try to recapture the happy companionship of their day out. But a question was niggling at him. Why had Victoria gone along with her mother's idea that it was Edward's idea to send the food? As though reading his mind, Victoria's explanation rushed out.

'I really can't thank you enough for the food. I don't know how I shall be able to ever repay you.'

Something about the formal way she spoke, annoyed Andrew.

'There's no need to repay me. I did it for Alexander.'

Taken aback, Victoria said the first thing that came to mind and then immediately regretted it.

'He likes you. He's always scribbling away, like Drew, as he calls you.'

He turned to her, smiling with delight.

'Does he really like me?'

She nodded but then not wanting him to take this as an invitation to call more often, she added, 'But then he's a friendly child.'

'That's put me in my place, on a level with the milkman or postman.'

Hearing the bitterness in his voice and remembering his kindness, Victoria tried to make amends.

'They don't draw beautifully.'

'I wish others thought I drew beautifully then I'd sell more work.'

'Couldn't you hold an exhibition?'

'To begin with I'd need to have enough work of a high standard to interest a gallery, and that I haven't got. What I really want to paint needs larger canvases and I haven't room for that.'

'There'd be plenty of room in Upper House.'

'You must be joking! Grandfather thinks I'm a wastrel so he wouldn't do anything to help me.'

'It's such a pity. He really does miss so much by avoiding being close to people.'

'So do you.'

The words fell like a stone in a pond, their thoughts spreading out like ripples. They both knew Andrew was meaning Victoria's self-imposed emotional isolation and all that implied. The silence grew until neither knew how to break it. Victoria longed to retrace her steps, to go back into the secure walls of the house, leaving Andrew to continue alone. But then she remembered his kindness to her son. So she waited with him on the platform until the train came in and then because it seemed churlish to just walk away, she hovered uncertainly whilst Andrew stood at the compartment window.

A little farther down the train a couple were oblivious to stares as they embraced awkwardly through the window. Andrew leaned farther out to make himself heard above the noise of the steam engine, saying something about Alexander. She wanted to draw away, but his recent words about her avoiding closeness with people had stung her. She would show him she was human after all. Suddenly, she stood on tiptoe, brushing his cheek with a kiss. Then, pausing briefly, she looked at him challengingly, before turning to walk away, with no backward glance.

Fingers touching where her lips had been, Andrew watched her go. Would he ever understand her?

After kissing Andrew, Victoria walked very quickly out of the station but once outside, her spirits dropped and her pace slowed. Andrew hadn't said anything that she didn't already know, but it was quite another thing having it said to her face.

It wasn't that she wished she was involved more with people, for she still felt deeply dedicated to Philip's memory, but what was she inadvertently doing to

Alexander? Keeping herself aloof from men, was she denying him necessary male company? The last thing she wanted was for him to grow up a mummy's boy, unable to make his way in the world. But how could she bring men into her son's life without them thinking she had romantic designs?

Even when Alexander had completely recovered, Andrew called regularly at the little house in Ludlow. He always made out that he had some business there, paints or paper to buy, but Mrs Davey's sharp eyes noticed he frequently never carried anything.

'He's very fond of the boy,' she told Victoria. 'Most probably wishes he was his own.'

'Well, then, he should marry,' Victoria replied, but at the same time her heart lurched a little, for if Andrew did marry what would happen to his visits to Alexander?

With Alexander fit again, Victoria had gone looking for a job but the only work she could find was in the kitchen of a hotel. The manager had been very apologetic when he told her what was wanted was someone to clean and prepare vegetables for lunch time. But she jumped at the chance of supplementing her meagre income.

But working in the morning meant she sometimes wasn't at home when Andrew called. This didn't bother her, in fact it was a relief, but she could only hope her mother wasn't being tactless in some way. She shuddered to think about the heavy hints that might be dropped abut Andrew's lack of a son, and Alexander's lack of a father.

Victoria had been working at the hotel for nearly a month when the cook and maids were thrown into red-faced confusion by Andrew's appearance at the kitchen door. Attractive men of his obvious social background did not normally deign to visit these quarters! When he asked if Victoria had finished work, the cook was thrown into a quandary.

She knew there was still half a bucket

of carrots to peel, but on the other hand it would never do to have a gentleman hanging around the kitchen door. And if she asked him in, the giggling maids wouldn't do a stroke of work. So making it obvious that she was being magnanimous, she sent a girl to finish the vegetables and so allow Victoria to go early.

'You shouldn't have done that,' Victoria chided, once they were outside. 'I might lose my job.'

'I promise I won't do it again,' Andrew said, taking her by the elbow to steer her towards a tea-room.

'I can't go in there,' she protested. 'I'm dressed for work.'

'That's nothing to be ashamed of,' he replied firmly, but when they entered the tea-room Andrew protested firmly when they were steered towards a table in a dark corner.

'We'll sit here,' he said, heading for a more central table.

'You shouldn't have done that,' she whispered sharply as she sat down.

'Are you going to keep on saying, 'You shouldn't have done that,' all morning?' he asked, after ordering tea and cakes. 'Although I haven't actually done anything yet, I want to tell you some news.'

'You're having an exhibition,' she said, leaning forward excitedly.

'No, but it's something that will go a long way to making it a reality. My mother has offered me a room in her house. I've been to see it and it's the right size and the light's good.'

'Then what are you waiting for?'

He had hoped she would show some disappointment, regret at his going, but instead she was smiling, seemingly eager to hear more.

'Of course there are trains to Gloucester,' he said, waiting then for her to say she hoped he would come to see them.

'So will you keep your house in Lemster?' she asked.

'I don't know.'

His reply was so dull, almost sullen,

that she looked at him searchingly. There was something the matter. But what?

'Your grandfather isn't being awkward about it, is he?' she asked gently.

'He doesn't know, and anyway it's none of his business.'

She frowned, puzzled, sensing he wanted something from her. But what, she asked herself again.

'Alexander will miss you,' she said to break the silence.

'It's nice to be missed by someone, even though it's only a small boy.'

He looked at her intently, then seeing she wasn't going to challenge his words, he shrugged and got up.

'I must say goodbye to Alexander, perhaps try to explain to him why I won't be seeing him.'

His hand was on the table, steadying himself, and on the spur of the moment she covered it with hers.

'You could write to him, send him little drawings. He'd like that.'

'Perhaps you could write sometimes

to tell me how he's getting on.'

She nodded quickly, anything to get out of this uncomfortable situation.

A week later, Alexander was excited to receive a letter addressed just to him. The letter was short, simply written and after Victoria had read it to him a few times, Alexander knew it off by heart. There was also a drawing of a deer which Andrew said he had seen. This had to be pinned up in Alexander's room and within a week it was joined by another drawing, this time of a calf.

Mrs Davey tried to make much of Andrew's desire to keep in contact with the boy, but Victoria just shrugged and smiled, until her mother reminded her sharply that good manners meant she should reply on Alexander's behalf.

'I can't help the way you've shut yourself off since Philip died, but I'm not having it thought a daughter of mind lacks good manners.'

Sighing, Victoria went to reach down the pen and ink from the high shelf where it was kept out of the way of Alexander's inquisitive fingers.

'I'll get Alexander to draw a picture for you to enclose with your letter,' Mrs Davey said. 'Then he and I will go and post it. You'd like that, wouldn't you?' she asked the boy who immediately demanded paper and pencil. 'And if it wouldn't be too much trouble, could you send him my best wishes and say I hope he's settled in all right?'

Flushing, Victoria did so and reaching for an envelope hurriedly addressed and stamped it. Hopefully, once the letter was posted, her mother would let the subject of Andrew drop — until his next letter arrived.

9

It had soon become a daily ritual that when Alexander heard the postman's cheery whistle, he would run to the door, looking for a letter from Drew. As he couldn't tell if an envelope was addressed to him or not, he tended to tear open everything and run off with it.

Then an envelope arrived of such high-quality paper that his small fingers couldn't tear it. Hearing his exasperated cries, Victoria took it from him. At once she knew the sender. Edward Mansel used such stationary. Sending the disappointed boy away, she slowly opened the envelope and took out the single sheet of heavy, white notepaper

Dear Mrs Hampton,

I have an insurmountable problem and would be obliged if you would call at your earliest convenience to discuss

your re-employment.

Edward Mansel.

She read the letter several times before showing it to her mother.

'What do you make of this?' she asked, handing her mother her reading glasses. 'I wonder what the problem is?'

'Does it matter what it is? You've as good as got your job back! Mind you, it's taken him long enough to realise he can't manage without you.'

'How do I know he won't sack me again over the slightest thing?'

'You'll just have to keep him sweet, won't you?'

Then seeing Victoria's stubborn look, Mrs Davey dealt her ace card.

'It's nearly autumn and Alexander has outgrown all of last winter's clothes. If he isn't wrapped up warm and has nourishing food, goodness knows what he'll go down with. He might seem to have recovered from the measles but it always leaves a weakness.'

Her mother's words made an impact.

She would never forgive herself if Alexander should fall ill because she hadn't enough money to care for him properly.

Victoria went to Lemster the following afternoon. On the train she steeled herself to ignore any unpleasant comments Edward Mansel might make. She needed the money and so she would have to guard her tongue, mask her feelings with a non-committal expression.

When Mrs Pritchard opened the door of Upper House, she almost dragged Victoria inside.

'Welcome back. It's good to see you again. Is your little lad well? When you've finished with him,' she said, nodding towards the study door, 'come into the kitchen and have something to eat before you go back.'

Smiling her thanks, Victoria obeyed Edward Mansel's abrupt command to come in. To her surprise the room was brightly lit, almost dazzlingly so. Even though it took a few seconds for her eyes to adjust to the light, she saw Edward's swift movement as he put down a magnifying glass.

'Sit down,' he ordered, indicating the chair by the desk she had used before. 'I'll come straight to the point. Many of the notes I made years ago have faded and it's taking me too long to decipher them. My publisher is after me to get this book finished and so I'm prepared to take you back.'

Victoria had to hold her breath to trap the indignant reply that had welled up at his attitude and high-handedness but then remembering Alexander's well-being depended on the better money Edward paid, she released her tension in a short sigh.

'When do you want me to start?'

'I don't suppose you thought to bring any clothes with you?'

'No, and I've my notice to serve.'

'Notice? What notice?'

'I can't leave my present employers in the lurch. I'll come in a week's time.'

'I suppose that will have to do,' was the ungracious reply as Victoria rose to leave.

Going into the kitchen, she smiled. She didn't have to give a week's notice. The hotel wouldn't have any difficulty in finding someone else. Making Edward wait was a small but satisfying victory.

As soon as Victoria opened the door of her mother's house, she was taken aback by the happy noise. Above Alexander's excited shrieking she could hear another voice, Andrew's! Tired after her journey, she paused for a moment. In the house she normally relaxed, could be herself, but now she would have to put up the defences she used to shield herself from others. Taking a deep breath, she opened the living-room door, her smile fixed.

'Well, how did you get on then?' Mrs Davey demanded. Then seeing Victoria's frown, she added, 'I've told Andrew all about it.'

'You had no right to discuss my

business.' Then seeing a shadow of hurt on Andrew's face, she added hurriedly, 'Sorry, but I'm tired. Mr Mansel was difficult as usual.'

'But you're back working for him?' Mrs Davey asked sharply.

When Victoria nodded, she softened. 'Sit down and tell us about it.'

'There's nothing to tell, except Mr Mansel has cataracts and so his sight is poor and on top of that, the publisher is after him to finish the book.'

Then turning to Andrew, she asked, 'Did you know about your grandfather's sight?'

He nodded.

'Grandfather won't have told you all that. Was it Mrs Pritchard? She also wrote to my mother. As grandfather never writes to her, Mrs Pritchard did. Not wanting to give away who had told her, Mother sort of dropped in last week but of course that old devil guessed. He nearly sent Mrs Pritchard packing, but Mother managed to make him see sense.'

'About me, too?' Victoria asked.

'She did tell him that if he persisted in getting rid of everyone around him, one day he would find himself totally alone.'

'So I've your mother to thank.'

'No, not really. From what I can gather, he was sorry before you were halfway to the station the day you left.'

'He could have said.'

'That isn't his way, is it? But few of us are entirely open when it comes to our behaviour, are we?'

There was something in Andrew's penetrating glance that made Victoria hastily turn the conversation on to safer ground.

'How's your painting going?' she asked. 'Have you completed enough pictures for an exhibition?'

'That will take some time. I want to try to show the beauty of our part of England through four seasons, so I've a long way to go yet.'

Victoria was genuinely interested but

before she could ask any more questions, Alexander demanded attention from his Drew.

On the agreed day, Victoria caught a very early train to Lemster. It had been hard leaving Alexander again, especially as he had become used to her being home with him. Lying awake the previous night, she let her thoughts wander to what, in reality, was impossible.

One day she would have enough money to be able to look after Alexander properly, without going out to work. She would own a bookshop, or perhaps run a small guest house. She fell asleep reminding herself sternly that these were only fantasies, that it was wiser to live day to day with no dreams that could be shattered as her life had been when Philip was killed.

After just a few hours in Upper House, Victoria felt she had never been away, except now she had to read notes aloud for Edward instead of just handing them to him. He never mentioned his eyesight and nor did she, but there were times when his obvious irritability at having to depend on her took all of her patience. But despite the difficulties, his book was going well and one afternoon he mentioned the illustrations it would need.

'I did a few sketches years ago. I wonder where they are? Do you think you could look in the large box on the top shelf?'

Sneezing loudly from the dust, Victoria reached down the dilapidated box which collapsed as she put it on his desk. As a cascade of sketches and small water colours slid out, she spoke without thinking.

'Now I know where Andrew gets his artistic skills.'

Picking up his magnifying glass to study a sketch more closely, Edward's reply was frosty.

'This was a hobby. To keep a wife and family, I wrote and lectured.'

Knowing he was getting at Andrew, Victoria asked, 'Wasn't writing a precarious way of making a living?'

'No, I made quite sure I had a decent, regular income from several sources before I took on any responsibilities.'

'Andrew is able to take his painting very seriously now he's living with his mother and has a decent studio there.'

'My daughter-in-law never told me. How long has this been going on?' he demanded.

She wanted to tell him that as he had banished Andrew from his life then he could hardly expect to be informed of everything that happened, but instead she told him of Andrew's plans for an exhibition.

'One exhibition, even if it does take place, is hardly a career,' he replied.

'Money isn't everything.'

'I'm surprised to hear you of all people say that, when money has brought you back here.'

As they faced each other across the desk, Victoria's angry gaze suddenly softened with thoughts of Alexander.

'As you well know, I have a son to support. If there had been another way of earning a living I wouldn't be here now.'

Then seeing him open his mouth no doubt in anger, she silenced him with a raised hand as she continued.

'But let's face facts. You and I need each other. You need my eyes and I need the money you pay me.'

To her surprise, he nodded, his stern mouth lifting slightly in a smile.

'You're right, of course. As our disagreements seem to stem from my grandson, for future harmony his name will not be mentioned.'

There was something about his words that sent a cascade of cold shivers down Victoria's back. Names identified people and Edward's words seemed to erase Andrew.

Much to Victoria's relief, during the week, Alexander soon settled down again with his grandmother. But Victoria was worried, for Andrew now took to visiting Ludlow a couple of times a week, when she wasn't there. What was he trying to do? Was he driving a wedge between her and Alexander, being the one to turn up when the boy was bored?

And why didn't Andrew come at weekends when he knew she would be there? Was he avoiding her?

In the quiet of her room at Upper House, these thoughts went round and round her head and gained more dark strength. She half wondered whether to talk to Mrs Pritchard who seemed to know Andrew better than anyone else. But she decided against this, for to confide in anyone meant lowering her defences, and that she would never do.

Then Mrs Davey, with little tact, asked Victoria why, if he was there on a Friday, Andrew made a point of hurrying away before she arrived from Lemster? She had even asked him to stay for an early supper, but he had hurried away before Victoria's usual time for coming home. Dropping wearily into a chair and kicking off her serviceable shoes, Victoria held out her arms to Alexander. But instead of rushing for a cuddle as usual, the boy sulked, dark rings of tiredness around his eyes.

'How long has he been like this?' Victoria demanded, leaning forward to put a hand on his forehead.

'He's been as right as rain. Andrew will have tired him out.'

'Andrew! Andrew! I'm sick of hearing his name. Anyone would think he lived here the way he seems to be the centre of your conversation.'

'You should be grateful he takes such an interest in the boy.'

'Why? Why should I be grateful? Before Andrew came on the scene you and Alexander were perfectly happy.'

'Alexander is older. He needs a man's company.'

'What rot! At his age it doesn't matter if he's with women all the time.'

'How can you say that? If you could

see Andrew and Alexander together, even you would understand what I mean.'

'Are you saying I'm deliberately avoiding something?'

Knowing that what she wanted to say might cause a row, Mrs Davey paused. Then deciding the evening was already soured, she continued.

'You know you are. Going through life avoiding men might be your way of dealing with Philip's death, but what right have you to inflict the same thing on Alexander? It gives me no pleasure at all to say this, but you're going the right way to becoming a bitter, friendless woman.'

'I'm not bitter or friendless.'

'Aren't you? If nothing else, try to be honest. Where have all your friends got to? This house was always full of girls dropping in.'

'They've grown up and have families.'

'You mean some of them have husbands who've returned from the war. From what I've seen, you've made those poor girls feel guilty about it. And as for the ones who are in the same boat as you, they've got on with life.'

'So have I. I'm working to support Alexander.'

'I mean life to do with people. I was very ashamed of your hard look and silence when Mary Bailey said she was remarrying. Oh, you wished her well all right but you forced it out, your throat tight with disapproval. With every passing month, you've dragged your martyrdom closer around you.'

Standing up, Victoria grabbed Alexander's hand and half dragging him from the room, she hurled over her shoulder, 'I love Philip and always will.'

'In that case, all I can say is heaven help you, and however much it displeases you, I shall continue to welcome Andrew here for the child's sake.'

10

True to her words, Victoria's mother welcomed Andrew to the house and as though to reinforce her welcome, she always saw to it that he shared a meal with her and Alexander. Mrs Davey often had a lump in her throat when she saw Andrew and Alexander together. Much as she liked and admired Andrew, life would have been fairer if it had been Philip playing with the boy, showing him things and disciplining gently. But that was not to be.

Andrew always asked about Victoria, how she was getting on with his grandfather and he was obviously pleased that all seemed well there. Yet despite his interest, he seemed intent on not meeting her, and Mrs Davey often muttered to herself at the stubbornness of the two of them.

Mrs Davey never mentioned Andrew's visits to Victoria but she found out from Alexander's childish chatter that he and Drew had been drawing, been for a walk, or had told him a story. As Victoria saw it, she was caught in a trap one set by her mother with the connivance of Andrew. If she said Andrew wasn't to visit again, how could she explain this to Alexander?

The boy had already realised he hadn't a father like others and to suddenly take away the man he had grown so fond of might harm him. So despite mounting irritation and anxiety that she was no longer in sole charge of her son, she decided to wait a week or two to see if with the coming of winter Andrew's visits would lessen and hopefully stop.

One autumn Saturday morning the firm sound of the door knocker sent Alexander running, quickly followed by Victoria. So at last Andrew had the courage to visit whilst she was at home. Pulling open the door, her face set, she restrained her excited son. It would be difficult to be cool with Andrew if Alexander had flung himself at him. But to Victoria's surprise and Alexander's disappointment, it was not Andrew on the doorstep.

Removing his bowler hat, Edward Mansel greeted her politely!

'I hope I haven't called at an inconvenient time.'

As Alexander hid behind her skirt, Victoria's mind whirled. What did Edward Mansel want? Why hadn't he said yesterday that he would be calling? Should she ask him in?

'I thought it time I met the boy,' Edward said, looking down at Alexander with the merest hint of a smile.

'Come in.'

Standing to one side, Victoria breathed a sigh of relief that her mother always went out on a Saturday morning to visit a friend. At least they would be spared any forthright, tactless comments. In the living-room, Edward stood uncertainly, looking straight ahead. It was then

139

Victoria's astonishment gave way to compassion. Poor man. He didn't know what to do or say.

'Do sit down,' she said with a smile, and as he gingerly obeyed, choosing an uncomfortable straight-back chair, she continued, 'I didn't know you were coming to Ludlow.'

Balancing his bowler hat on his knee, Edward seemed to be having difficulty in meeting Victoria's eye.

'I'm on my way to visit Howard Reece and as I'm early for my appointment I thought I would call to pay my respects to your mother and also meet your son.'

Alexander had now retreated behind his mother's chair.

'I'm sorry, but my mother's out,' Victoria replied. 'Alexander, come here and say hello to Mr Mansel.'

Ignoring Edward's outstretched hand, the boy came reluctantly to stand by his mother.

'He's a little young to be shaking hands,' Victoria explained, pushing

Alexander forward a little. 'Say hello to Mr Mansel.'

Alexander's silence was accompanied by an unblinking stare which obviously made Edward feel uncomfortable. During a silence that seemed as long as an hour, Victoria willed Edward to speak and Alexander to behave in his normal friendly way. But they continued to look suspiciously at each other.

'Would you like a cup of tea?' Victoria offered hurriedly.

'No, thank you. I don't drink tea at this time of the morning.'

'Of course,' she said lamely.

Silence followed again. She glanced at the clock on the mantelpiece. What time was his meeting with Mr Reece? Edward was always precise, so it would be either on the hour or half past.

'Perhaps I'm keeping you from something,' Edward said with formal politeness, but he made no move to leave.

'No.'

Although the clock's ticking seemed to fill the room, it appeared to be going slower and slower. Removing an impressive gold repeater watch from his waistcoat pocket, Edward checked it against the clock.

'I think your clock is a trifle slow,' he said, then with a slight smile he added, 'We don't want you missing your train on Monday morning, do we?'

But Victoria didn't reply, for with eyes firmly fixed on the watch, Alexander crossed to stand in front of Edward. Victoria waited, curious to see what would happen. Would Edward do the normal thing of showing the child the watch?

'Here,' Edward said and slowly held out the watch. 'See, if I pull this, it will strike the last hour so I know roughly what time it is.'

Fascinated, Alexander moved closer as Edward demonstrated the watch's chiming. Then as though remembering something dragged back from distant memories, Edward held the watch towards Alexander's ear.

'Do you want to hear it tick?'

The boy moved closer and as he listened intently, he put a hand on Edward's knee. Victoria held her breath. How would Edward react to such familiarity? But seeming to be taken with Alexander's obvious fascination, he appeared not to notice. But like all small children, Alexander's attention soon switched to something else and his shyness now less, he didn't hesitate before touching Edward's bowler hat.

'Don't!' Victoria ordered, leaning forward to stop him.

His always sticky hands would spoil the fabric's pile.

'It's all right.'

She could hardly believe her ears. Edward was allowing a small boy to handle a personal possession! Then her amazement was further fuelled when Edward suddenly put the bowler on Alexander's head.

'It's a little big for you,' he said,

as Alexander peered up at him from under the brim.

Then with a swiftness that caught Edward unawares, Alexander took off the hat and held it in front of his face.

'Boo!' '

As Alexander peeped around the hat, his childish shout startled Edward who looked hurriedly at Victoria.

'It's a game,' she said, then wondering how Edward would react she said, 'If you say 'Boo' back . . . '

'Boo,' Edward replied but without the usual force, Alexander frowned.

'Boo!' the boy tried again, moving the hat rapidly.

'That's enough. Give the hat back to Mr Mansel,' Victoria ordered.

Poor man, he was well out of his depth. Hadn't he ever played with children, with Andrew? As Alexander cautiously obeyed, Edward spoke almost apologetically.

'I'm not used to children.'

How sad, Victoria thought.

'I find playing with him relaxes me,' she said gently.

Edward smiled thinly.

'So you need to relax after working for me?'

'I didn't mean that,' she flustered. 'We all have a bit of the child in us and playing with them brings back that carefree time.'

'Your generation is most fortunate. I was brought up to be seen and not heard. We were little adults. I wouldn't have dared to take someone's hat.'

'Oh, I'm sorry!'

'Don't be. It was pleasant to see the boy's curiosity, and with the watch, but I must be going. Perhaps I might have the pleasure of meeting your mother another time.'

Having made up his mind to leave, Edward Mansel was through the door almost before Victoria had time to realise what was happening.

'Goodbye,' she said to his rapidly retreating back.

Then, as she shut the door, she

shook her head in puzzlement. How very strange. Edward Mansel was the last person to go dropping in uninvited, and as he never did anything without a purpose, she wondered what he was up to. When Mrs Davey returned, she was very vexed that she had missed such an important visitor but unlike Victoria, she immediately came up with the reasons for Edward Mansel's visit.

'Perhaps he was giving your home life the once-over,' she decided.

'Why on earth should he want to do that? After all I've been working for him for long enough.'

'Does he know Andrew comes here often?'

'I haven't told him and as far as I know he's still not talking to Andrew.'

'Ah, but perhaps . . . '

'Perhaps what?' Victoria snapped. 'My, you do like mysteries when none exists.'

'I was just thinking. If Mr Mansel feels Andrew needs steadying down, then he might be thinking the

146

responsibilities of a family would do it.'

For a moment Victoria frowned, then as the implications of her mother dawned on her, anger coloured her cheeks and sharpened her voice.

'Andrew does not need steadying down. He's a brilliant artist and all this talk of art not being a proper job makes me sick. And if you're thinking what I think you're thinking, then you're going soft in the head. If Mr Mansel was looking for a bride for Andrew then he'd be aiming a lot higher than someone like me.'

To ease the tension Mrs Davey added with a chuckle, 'Of course it might not be Andrew he was thinking about. You know the saying about being an old man's darling.'

'Now I know for sure you've gone soft in the head,' Victoria declared.

But when she returned to Upper House the following Monday, Mrs Pritchard could hardly wait for her to get inside before she launched into conversation.

'You never said Mr Mansel was going to visit you. He seems very taken with Alexander. I never would have believed it. It's a pity he didn't show that much interest in his own flesh and blood. Still, anything that will make him more human must be good.'

As Mrs Pritchard took a deep breath ready for more questioning, Victoria neatened her hair and made for the study door.

'You know what Mr Mansel is like about punctuality. If I'm late, liking Alexander or not, he'll give me my marching orders again.'

But it was with reluctance that Victoria entered the study. What on earth was going on? Life was getting so complicated, what with Andrew and now Edward Mansel showing an interest in her family. She needed to be firmly in charge of her life and Alexander's, but with the two Mansel men seeming to be intent in involving themselves, she felt both vulnerable and angry.

To Victoria's great relief Edward Mansel didn't mention his visit to Ludlow or Alexander. But there was a subtle change in him. He was less terse and withdrawn and this made working with him far more agreeable. She was just beginning to think Edward's visit had been spontaneous, something he was no doubt regretting, when he surprised her yet again.

It was on the Tuesday of the following week when he said abruptly, 'Has the boy ever been to Lemster?'

Puzzled, she shook her head.

'I would like your mother and the boy to come to tea on Friday. Your mother could look at the market first. I believe women enjoy such things. Then you could all return to Ludlow in the evening. Well?'

'I don't know what to say.'

'Has the boy ever been on a train?'

'His name is Alexander,' she prompted whilst shaking her head.

'The experience will be good for him,' Edward said as though an expert on children. 'He seems intelligent and so his mind needs stretching.'

Victoria opened her mouth to challenge him, to ask how he knew Alexander was intelligent, though of course she knew he was, but she shut it again.

Thinking her hesitation was because of the expense, Edward added gruffly, 'Of course as my guests I will pay their expenses.'

'There's no need,' Victoria replied stiffly. 'You pay me very well.'

'Victoria, you should know me by now. Once I've made up my mind, I don't like disagreement.'

'I'll have to ask my mother,' Victoria smiled faintly.

What a pair her mother would make with Edward Mansel, for they were both strong-headed and to varying degrees, manipulative.

Mrs Davey needed no persuading to come to Lemster and so on the Friday afternoon Victoria met her and Alexander at the station. The boy was jumping with excitement. Victoria led them to the market but after a quick look, Mrs Davey was eager to go to Upper House. Knowing Edward had asked Mrs Pritchard to prepare afternoon tea for half-past three, Victoria refused to return too early for that would give her mother even more time to put her foot in it.

When Mrs Pritchard let them in, Victoria was worn out. She took a steadying breath, for the worst was yet to come. Shutting her eyes briefly she sent up a silent prayer that her mother would for once be tactful, that Alexander would behave and Edward would be . . . well, what did she want Edward to be? Interested in Alexander? Eager to talk to her mother?

'Mr Mansel is in the morning-room.'

Mrs Pritchard's words snapped Victoria out of her daze.

'The morning-room?' she repeated. 'I've never known it to be used.'

'It hasn't been for years. No need with him almost living in that study

151

of his. But he said it would be better for Alexander.'

Here, Mrs Pritchard looked down at the child as though wondering what magic there was about him that had changed Mr Mansel.

'You're a fine-looking boy,' she said. 'I've made some toffee if you want to come into the kitchen after your tea. Perhaps you'd like to come, too,' Mrs Pritchard asked Mrs Davey pleasantly.

Victoria vowed to be there as well, for if Mrs Pritchard thought she would be able to winkle out information from her mother, then she had met her match. It would be a meeting of experts.

When they went into the morning-room, Victoria gasped in astonishment for as well as the groaning tea table, there were building bricks, a wooden fort, tin soldiers and a magnificent, if battered rocking horse that brought an exclamation of delight from Alexander. Silent with surprise, Victoria played no part in the conversation which seemed to be flowing with astonishing ease between Edward and her mother.

By the look of the toys, they had obviously been in the family for many years. But why had Edward taken the trouble of bringing them from the attic, when they might have held painful memories of children long gone and with whom he was never at ease?

Just then Mrs Pritchard came in with the teapot and hot-water jug and after an enquiring glance, put them within Mrs Davey's reach. Sitting slightly to one side with Alexander, Victoria watched her mother revel in the rôle of hostess. It was almost as though Victoria wasn't there, for, apart from necessary questioning about whether she or Alexander wanted anything, the conversation flowed around her.

It was strange to sit there and hear Edward's polite questions and her mother's answers, especially when most of the time they were talking about her. But whether it was because she was busy watching Alexander eating before hurrying back to the toys, Victoria felt no urge to join in, even though normally she would have objected most hotly to being talked about.

As in dreams, time seemed to fly and soon it was time for them to leave for the train. Clutching a bag of Mrs Pritchard's toffee, Alexander chattered excitedly about the wonderful toys as he walked between his mother and grandmother. Raising her voice to be heard over him, Mrs Davey wondered why Edward Mansel had gone to so much trouble and wasn't he fond of Alexander and of Victoria? Mrs Davey gave her daughter a questioning look.

'Fond of me? Don't be so ridiculous. I work for him, remember?'

'Don't tell me all employers go to so much trouble,' Mrs Davey snorted. 'I'm telling you there's something behind all of this.'

'Can't you just accept he might be just a lonely old man?'

Mrs Davey nodded triumphantly.

'And lonely old men might suddenly

discover what they've missed in life.
That's a big house.'

Victoria was thankful that once on
the train, Alexander fell asleep so
stopping any further conversation.

11

That weekend Victoria's mood was so volatile that her mother eventually spoke to her sharply.

'Whatever's got into you? You've done nothing but snap at me and now Alexander can do nothing right. If you go on like this, we'll both be glad to see the back of you when Monday comes.'

'You're hedging me in.'

'Hedging you in? What on earth do you mean?'

'You, Andrew, Mr Mansel, you're all driving me into a corner. You all seem to think you know what's best for me but the only one who knows that is me and the sooner you all realise that, the better.'

Hoping to calm Victoria down, Mrs Davey's tone was gentle.

'All right, I know I tend to organise

you, but I cannot for the life of me fathom what you have against Andrew and Mr Mansel.'

'Andrew comes here often, doesn't he? And, when I'm not here. And why is Edward Mansel taking such an interest in us all of a sudden?'

'You should be glad Andrew is spending time with Alexander. Boys need a man in their life if they're not to be soft. And as for Mr Mansel, can't you accept he's concerned about you?'

'You don't know Edward like I do. He never does anything without good reason and as he's alienated his own family, I want to know why he's showing such an interest in mine.'

'He could be regretting falling out with Andrew.'

'Then let him make it up with Andrew and not meddle in my life.'

'For Alexander's sake, you know you can't afford to rub Mr Mansel up the wrong way, so you'll just have to accept any interest he shows in you or Alexander. As for Andrew, with winter coming and him being busy with his painting, well, that situation might soon resolve itself, and I just hope it's not for the worse.'

Much to Victoria's relief Edward Mansel didn't mention Alexander or her mother. She wouldn't have thought him one to have passing fancies but meeting her family must have been just that. However, Mrs Pritchard wouldn't let the subject drop until Victoria told her sharply that she didn't want to hear another word about it. This led to a strained atmosphere and so although the evenings were drawing in, Victoria looked forward to her walk after she had posted her daily letter to Alexander.

One Thursday evening, hearing hurrying footsteps behind her, Victoria knew without looking around that it was Polly.

'Hello, Victoria. I'm just off to see old Ben. He's gone and fallen again. I've so much to do, I don't know which way to turn. If you've a minute or two, do you think you could help me out?'

'Of course,' Victoria agreed readily. 'What can I do?'

Trying to keep up with her and in the fading light, Victoria didn't notice where they were going until Polly suddenly stopped. With a hand to her heaving chest, she gasped.

'Andrew's come back and his neighbour, Mrs Hedges, says he's been shut in there for a couple of days now. I'm worried he's ill or that mother of his has fallen out with him. Will you go in and see what's happened?'

Quickly opening the gate to Rose Cottage, Polly not only pushed Victoria through, but waited to see she knocked on the door. She needed to escape, but where could she go? The door opened with swift suddenness and she stood there frozen, silent.

'Victoria, what's the matter? You look awful. Is Alexander all right?'

Taking her arm, Andrew pulled her inside.

'Alexander's fine,' she heard herself say as though from a great distance.

He turned towards the living-room, obviously expecting her to follow, but she stood rooted to the spot. If she followed, she would have to say something, but what? Realising she was still in the tiny hall, Andrew turned awkwardly, a fleeting shadow of pain quickly replaced by concern.

'There is something the matter, isn't there? Is it Grandfather? He hasn't sacked you again, has he?'

Shaking her head, she went reluctantly into the room.

'Polly . . .'

'So she's behind this!' he interrupted with a laugh.

Then just as suddenly his face set into hard lines.

'I might have guessed you wouldn't have come here of your own free will.'

Victoria took a deep breath to banish the last of her confusion, then back in total control, she squared her shoulders as she retorted, 'You're a fine one to talk! Most of the time you come to see Alexander when you know I'm not there.'

His nod of agreement was matched by a slight smile. Then indicating a chair, that she should sit down, he sank down wearily. She sat opposite him at the table which was, as usual, littered with sketches and paints.

'Is there something wrong at your mother's? The exhibition hasn't fallen through, has it?'

'Would you care if it had?'

'Of course I would. You've great talent, Andrew.'

'I suppose that's praise coming from you,' he muttered, then he seemed to force himself to look at her directly. 'Victoria, what's going on between you and Grandfather?'

Dumbfounded, she could only stare at him in bewilderment.

'Mrs Pritchard wrote to me,' he went on.

'So she spies for you, does she?' Victoria accused.

'It isn't like that. She thought I

161

should know about your mother and Alexander coming to Upper House.'

'Why? What's it to her, or you? If you and Edward have fallen out, I really don't see that what he does is any concern of yours.'

Now his anger matched hers.

'So it's Edward now, is it? And you're certainly quick to leap to his defence. So I repeat, what's going on between you?'

Then as the full impact of his question hit her, Victoria sat back.

'If you're implying what I think you are, you've a very nasty mind. Mr Mansel,' and she put a very heavy emphasis on his name, 'is my employer, nothing more.'

'I've never known Grandfather show interest even in his own family.'

'Perhaps he has regrets. Perhaps old age is mellowing him. He seems quite content with his life.'

'So being an old man's darling . . . '

Andrew never finished the saying for Victoria broke into laughter.

'You really don't think your grand-father is thinking of asking me to marry him, do you? Can you really see him choosing someone as strong-willed as me? And what about Alexander? Can you imagine him running around Upper House?'

'I suppose not,' was the muttered reply.

Then as a new thought occurred to Victoria, her face hardened.

'Were you frightened you might lose out if Edward did ask me to marry him?'

Andrew brought the flat of his hand down on the table so sharply, that a jam jar of pencils rattled.

'As far as I'm concerned, he can take his money to the grave with him. You really don't understand, do you? It's you, Victoria, it's you. Haven't you realised I care for you? That's why I've come back. Though what I thought I could have done about it, if you and Grandfather . . . ' He tailed off, looking down at his hands.

'I've made a fool of myself, haven't I? About you and Grandfather?' he asked with weary certainty.

Leaning across the table, she put her hand over his.

'No, no you haven't, but you must admit it's so improbable.'

Swiftly he moved his hands, capturing hers.

'Jealousy can make a man think and do strange things.'

The tension between them was now so charged, Victoria hardly dared to breath. She knew they were both on the edge of something and she couldn't see how to draw back.

'I love you, Victoria.'

It was said softly. Then raising his head, he repeated it loudly and firmly.

'I love you.'

Heart hammering, Victoria was stunned.

'Well, in for a penny in for a pound,' Andrew said with a wry smile. 'Victoria, will you marry me?'

As though hypnotised, she stared at

him. She seemed to have lost the power of speech, of making sense of the words flying around in her head.

'You don't love me,' he said flatly.

'I . . . '

She had been going to say, 'I don't,' when something stopped her.

'I don't know,' she trailed off.

What was she saying? Why hadn't she spoken the truth, said he was just a friend?

Seizing the chance to make an important point, Andrew said swiftly, 'Alexander needs a father.'

Those four words brought her back to what she called reality.

'Philip is his father,' she said coldly.

Andrew flinched as though she had struck him, but he continued quietly.

'I don't want to usurp Philip, just be a substitute, albeit possibly a poor one at times. I'm fond of Alexander and I think he is of me.'

'That's a poor reason for marrying me,' she countered.

'You haven't been listening to me,

have you? Victoria, I love you. I want you to be my wife. I know I'm not much of a catch,' and here he slapped his lame leg in anger, 'but surely it's what's in my heart that matters. Tell me honestly, what's in your heart? Do you care enough to marry me?'

She spoke slowly.

'Philip and I had loved each other almost from being children. I've never felt anything for another man. I don't know if I could love someone else, if I'm capable of loving. I feel dead inside.'

They sat either side of the table, not touching, Victoria avoiding Andrew's compassionate eyes.

'Will you think about it?' he asked eventually.

'Surely love isn't thought about? she replied. 'I didn't have to think about whether I loved Philip or not.'

'Like I didn't have to think about whether I loved you.'

She bit her lip. She might not know whether she was able to love again, but she did realise Andrew meant what he had said and in doing so had made himself vulnerable. She didn't want to hurt him but . . .

Seeing her indecision, Andrew spoke quickly.

'Will you at least think about it? I'd rather live in hope than despair.'

Rising hurriedly, she nodded.

'I must go. Edward, Mr Mansel, will soon be locking up.'

As he opened the door for her, she smiled at him fleetingly.

'Victoria, don't run away from me. And if it's not to be me, don't run away from life,' she heard him say softly.

12

Victoria spent a sleepless night, and the following morning at breakfast, her mood was not improved by Mrs Pritchard's obvious inquisitiveness.

'Polly's just told me you called on Andrew last night.'

Refusing the scrambled eggs, Victoria nodded curtly. How much did Polly and Mrs Pritchard guess about what had happened?

'I wonder what's brought Andrew back? Is he all right?'

'Yes.'

Then taking a hasty gulp of tea, Victoria pushed back her chair and left without her usual smiling thanks.

If Edward found Victoria more preoccupied than usual, he didn't remark on it. She was as efficient as usual, and eager to finish his book. He, too, gave their work all his attention. But in the kitchen, Polly and Mrs Pritchard speculated about what might have occurred between Victoria and Andrew.

But they soon discovered they had more questions than answers. Then the butcher's boy, calling with the order, mentioned he had seen Andrew hurrying in a black mood to the station. But they were not to be thwarted and Mrs Pritchard resolved that evening to ask Victoria into the kitchen for a cup of cocoa and so try to win her confidence.

Sorry for her morning brusqueness, Victoria accepted the invitation, though she guessed she would be in for another grilling, but this time she would be prepared. Going into the hot kitchen and being led firmly to the most comfortable chair by the fire, Victoria hid her smile as Mrs Pritchard put a cushion to her back.

'Comfy, dear?' she asked.

Sipping the hot, sweet cocoa, Victoria nodded. If Mrs Pritchard was trying to relax her tongue by warmth and comfort, then she could work it to her own advantage by pretending to be sleepy. But the housekeeper's first words brought her upright in her chair.

'It's a pity that fiancée of Andrew's threw him over.'

Seeing Victoria's reaction, Mrs Pritchard knew she had hit the bull's eye first time.

'You didn't know?'

'No, but then why should I?'

'I thought he might have mentioned it.'

'You only discuss that sort of thing with friends.'

'I thought you were friends.'

'No,' Victoria said very clearly as though to underline it. 'I know Andrew because he's Mr Mansel's grandson.'

It took all her willpower to meet Mrs Pritchard's quizzical gaze. How much did the housekeeper know about Andrew's visits to Ludlow? She barely suppressed a sigh. The day was ending as it had begun with Mrs Pritchard prying as she had expected, but what she hadn't expected was the discovery that Andrew had kept something from her. He had proposed to someone before her. He might treat marriage lightly, but she did not.

Victoria left the kitchen as quickly as she could and, full of righteous indignation, she decided to write Andrew a letter he wouldn't forget in a hurry. Later, she couldn't quite recall what she had written except that in harsh, terse words, she had accused him of not being open with her about his previous relationship. She ended by saying marriage had to be based on complete confidence between man and wife and he did not have hers.

Although Mr Mansel had long since locked up for the night, Victoria let herself out quietly. Such a letter had to be posted immediately and slipping it into the post box she told herself that now she would sleep better. Andrew had saved her the trouble of finding an excuse for her rejection of his proposal.

Although Victoria felt that as far as she was concerned, Andrew's proposal was now very firmly in the past, she knew he might well not let it go just like that. But by the time Wednesday of the following week had come with no reply from him, she began to relax. But at the same time she was pricked by a resentment that in her calmer moments she recognised to be unjustified. So he hadn't been serious after all. He had tried to use her for some spur-of-the moment flight of fancy. She had thought better of him, that he would have treated her more seriously.

But when, that morning, Mrs Pritchard brought in the post to Mr Mansel, she indicated by a quick jerk of her head that she wanted to see Victoria. So making some excuse, Victoria followed her into the hall where the housekeeper gave her a letter.

'I didn't give it to you in there

as Mr Mansel would have recognised Andrew's writing.'

Mrs Pritchard hovered, obviously keen to know more, but Victoria ran up the stairs to her room. Flopping down on the bed, she tore open the envelope with impatient, shaking fingers. Would his letter be angry, accusing? But as she skimmed it, growing discomfort enveloped her. In straightforward terms Andrew explained that his fiancée had broken off their engagement because she couldn't face marrying a disabled man. She abhorred physical scars and wanted her children to have a normal father.

He went on to say he realised Victoria also felt this way, too. Pity, anger, then shame for what she had written, reduced Victoria to tears. If Philip had come back with far worse injuries than Andrew, she would still have loved him. By thoughtlessly seizing on a seemingly easy way out, she had inflicted terrible hurt on Andrew, no doubt making him feel even more aware of his injuries. But could she make amends somehow? She could write yet again, try to explain that his physical state meant nothing to her, the reason for her refusal being . . . being what?

Suddenly standing up, she deliberately turned her thoughts to Alexander. She must return to the study, not give Edward Mansel a reason to accuse her of slacking. Deep down she knew she was being unjust to him, for since meeting her son and mother, he had begun to thaw, his conversation not always about his work. Crossing to the flowered water jug on the marble-topped wash-stand, she splashed cold water on to her face. She could write to Andrew later and explain. Then the words would come easier, her thoughts and feelings having had time to settle.

But Victoria left the writing of the letter for one day, then two, then three, four. It was so easy to let it slide away, excusing that to write would be to hurt Andrew even more. In the small hours of the morning when brutal honesty often haunted the sleepless, she knew shame that she couldn't write to him because she didn't know what to say.

Emotions swirled around her brain, her very being, until with hands pressed tightly over her eyes, she sobbed, wanting relief from this unasked-for complication. Although it had been hard, she had become used to the life she had created after Philip's death. In her thoughts, she determinedly tried to substitute Alexander's name for Andrew's. Her son was the only one who mattered. He had his whole life before him.

This time the letter from Andrew was sent to Ludlow. As her mother handed it to her, Victoria wondered grimly about Andrew's motives in sending it there. Had he thought that when her mother saw his letter, she would demand to know what had happened, force her to reply to him?

What Victoria didn't know was that Andrew had visited much less frequently to see Alexander and even then he hadn't stayed long, had seemed distracted. Noticing this, for once Mrs Davey had held her tongue, not wanting to add to whatever was troubling Andrew. Better he came infrequently than not at all. But her silence did not extend to Victoria.

'I knew something was the matter between you and Andrew and his letter proves it,' Mrs Davey said grimly. 'What have you done?'

'Why should it be me? I haven't done anything,' Victoria snapped back. 'Perhaps you should ask Andrew what it is he's done.'

But the way she coloured told her mother that she knew this to be unjust. Andrew hadn't done anything of which to be ashamed.

Softening a little, Mrs Davey asked, 'Aren't you going to read it? It might be important.'

Knowing she had no option, Victoria turned her back slightly as she opened the letter. Her hands shook as she skimmed the few words, then as their meaning sunk in, shame made her bite her lower lip. Andrew was thinking of her son, of what affect it might have when Andrew stopped seeing him, as in the circumstances he would have to do.

He suggested they met at Rose Cottage where they could agree on a satisfactory story to tell the boy. Andrew ended by saying that as she had not replied to his last letter, to save drawing out an unpleasant situation, he would be at Rose Cottage on Sunday evening and he hoped she would meet him there. He finished acknowledging that she might find this personally difficult, but Alexander had to come first.

'Well?' Mrs Davey demanded impatiently.

'Mother, I'm a grown woman now,' Victoria turned to face her. 'Can't I even have a letter without you prying?'

'You might be a grown woman but you're still my daughter and I know full well you've got a guilty conscience about something. You've lost Andrew's friendship now, haven't you? I really don't know what's to become of you. I just pray I live long enough to see that Alexander grows up to look forward to life, not be stunted by Philip's shadow like you are.'

If Mrs Davey hadn't been distracted by Alexander wanting a drink she might have seen the shadow of pain in Victoria's eyes.

★ ★ ★

By the time Victoria got out at Lemster station she could hardly contain her apprehension and what she saw as her righteous indignation. She was going to have to sit down with Andrew and calmly discuss Alexander. He was her son but she had been cornered into talking and listening to someone else about him. She tried to calm herself. Once a satisfactory story had been concocted to account for Andrew's withdrawal from Alexander's life, then Andrew would also withdraw from hers.

Raising her large black umbrella, she smiled grimly. The black skies and heavy downpour were certainly matching her mood. By the time she turned into Andrew's street, the heavy rain bouncing back from roads and pavement had drenched the bottom of her coat and skirt.

Holding her umbrella low, she knocked impatiently on Andrew's door. The least he could have done was watch out for her, be ready to open the door. She knocked again, louder this time in case the pounding rain had muffled her knock. Then she shivered, partly from the damp coldness and partly from the sudden certainty that the house was empty. Surely Andrew hadn't changed his mind, wasn't coming after all. Could he be that unthinking, uncaring?

Mounting irritation at being left in the rain drove her to peer into his living-room window and, seeing gentle flames lapping the coal in the grate, she sighed with relief. Perhaps he had gone out on some urgent errand, though what, she couldn't imagine. Perhaps Mrs Pritchard had done shopping for him and he had gone to Upper House to save her a wetting.

'Hurry up, Andrew!' she found herself muttering. 'Hurry up.'

She smiled wryly as she huddled in the meagre shelter of the doorway. One minute she hadn't wanted to meet him, the next she was eager for him to let her in. Then she remembered what Polly had told her about the hidden key, and hastily bending down she found its hiding place and let herself in.

In the tiny hallway she called out, but the only sound was a ticking clock and the sigh as embers settled in the fire. Taking off her coat and hat she shook off raindrops before hanging them on the hall stand. Andrew's coat wasn't there so he must be out.

Even though she knew he would have wanted her to go, Victoria went into the sitting-room very reluctantly. She valued her own privacy and here she was invading Andrew's. The warmth of the room reviving her, bringing back her usual determination, she went to the table. Perhaps he had left her a note, but there wasn't one. But then, she tried to excuse, if he had thought he would be back before she arrived, he wouldn't have written one.

Rubbing her hands together she crossed to the cheering fire. Then drawing a chair closer, she kicked off her wet shoes as she sat down.

She woke up with a start. How long had she been asleep? She couldn't remember even trying to fight off drowsiness. The room, gloomy before from the rain clouds, now had the blackness of approaching night. Getting up hurriedly, she peered at the clock on the mantelpiece. She had been asleep for over an hour, time enough for Andrew to have returned!

Not pausing to consider for even a second, she marched into the hall and grabbed her coat. So he had changed his mind, had he? And after all his protestations of not wanting Alexander to suffer! No doubt he had also changed his mind about her — two good reasons why he couldn't face her.

13

Her hat jammed on her head, anger making her fingers clumsy, Victoria had buttoned her coat crookedly but she didn't care. She had to get out of Andrew's house. Grabbing her umbrella from the drip tray of the hall stand, she opened the front door just as someone was knocking on it urgently.

'Victoria! There you are.'

Leaning against the door frame, Mrs Pritchard had her hand to her chest, obviously very distressed.

'Come in out of the rain,' Victoria urged, matching her words by pulling the housekeeper inside. 'What's wrong? Is Mr Mansel ill? How did you know I was here?'

'Andrew got in touch with me. He asked me to light a fire to air the place. He mentioned he was meeting

183

someone here. I reckoned it must be you.'

'Why did you think it would be me?' Victoria demanded — did half of Lemster know her business?

But with a curt wave of her hand, Mrs Pritchard silenced her.

'Is Andrew here?' she asked sharply, trying to look beyond Victoria into the living-room.

'No, he hasn't come.'

A hand to her mouth, Mrs Pritchard swayed back against the wall.

'I had hoped . . . '

'Hoped what? It's Andrew, isn't it? What's happened to him?'

Victoria took a step closer to her, sudden apprehension making her want to shake a swift reply from Mrs Pritchard.

'One of Polly's family is a porter at Lemster and when he called in to tell her there's been an accident, she came straight round to tell me. It seems the train's come off the track south of Dinmore Tunnel.'

'Is it the one Andrew would have been on?'

Mrs Pritchard nodded, adding grimly, 'People have been hurt.'

The two women looked at each other for a shared few seconds of apprehension. Then without a word, Victoria took off her coat and hat.

'I'll stay here,' she said. 'Does Mr Mansel know?'

'No, I thought it best if I came here first in case Andrew . . . '

'You had better get back to Upper House and tell Mr Mansel. If . . . if anything has happened, it will be him the police will tell.'

'You can't stay here alone. Come back with me,' Mrs Pritchard urged.

'No, I want to stay here. You know Andrew. He won't want any fuss. He'll just want to carry on as usual.'

The housekeeper headed back to Upper House. Closing the front door, Victoria wondered why she had said she wanted to stay when only minutes before she couldn't wait to leave.

But she refused to delve deep for an answer, concentrating instead on practical matters. Of course the fire would need tending, the room kept warm for Andrew's return. No trains would be running to Ludlow for some time, so it would be pointless going to the station, and going to Upper House would be to invite questions from Edward Mansel which she didn't want to answer.

But she wasn't to get off so lightly, for, minutes later, rushing with wildly beating heart in response to the door knocker, she found Edward Mansel standing there. Shocked by his pallor, the deeply-etched lines of worry on his face, she immediately stood aside for him to enter. He almost staggered as he crossed the threshold. Victoria guided him to a chair by the fire.

'Mrs Pritchard is going around like a headless chicken,' he gasped. 'I needed to be with someone calm. You think he's all right, Victoria?'

'Of course Andrew will be all right,'

she replied with forced confidence.

'He can't have come through the war to be . . . '

'We mustn't even think the worst,' she said firmly, kneeling down on the hearth rug.

'It's all my fault.' Edward's head dropped wearily. 'If only he hadn't gone to Gloucester.'

'If there's blame, then I'm guilty, too,' Victoria said slowly.

He looked up sharply but seeing her closed face, he didn't question. From what Mrs Pritchard had gabbled about Victoria being at Rose Cottage, he gathered something was going on between them.

'What a fool I've been,' he muttered. 'After meeting Alexander, I resolved to try to build bridges with Andrew. But you know how it is. There's always some reason why the next day would be better, or the next.'

How ironic, Victoria thought. Edward had wanted to build bridges and she had come intent on knocking down the one connecting Andrew to Alexander.

'What makes us act so stupidly?' Edward asked. 'The only family I have are Andrew and his mother and yet I've alienated them both. Learn from me, Victoria, and treasure your family and friends. I really do care for Andrew. I wanted the best for him, but he's stubborn.'

'I don't understand about you meeting Alexander. What has he to do with you and Andrew?'

'When I first saw the boy at your mother's house, I left feeling somehow lighter. It was as though he had blown away the cobwebs off my books.'

Embarrassed at having spoken of his feelings, Edward smiled apologetically.

'But it wasn't just Alexander. You've made a difference to Upper House. Suddenly I realised that for years I've been living in a self-made tomb.'

Deeply touched by his confession, Victoria leaned forward and clasped his cold, thin hand.

'Is that why you asked Mother and

Alexander to tea?' she asked gently.

He nodded.

'In my day, children were kept away from their parents, but I see now we need their excitement and joyfulness to keep a house alive. Alexander's delight at playing with the toys that day . . .'

He trailed off, looking down with surprise at their joined hands. Then as though gaining strength from the contact, he continued more firmly.

'I suppose I was hoping to replace Andrew with Alexander.'

Victoria's shock showed plainly on her face. Surely he hadn't meant to ask her to marry him? With a rare insight into another's feelings, Edward Mansel smiled wryly as he shook his head.

'No, Victoria, I know I'm a silly old fool but I'm not that silly. I'd hoped that occasionally Alexander would come to play with the toys.'

Pity touched Victoria's heart. Poor old man! He wanted a child's company but couldn't bring himself to make it on a personal level. The toys would be the reason for bringing Alexander to Upper House, not Edward himself.

'If you want it, I'll bring Alexander to visit you. He hasn't got a grandfather so in time . . .'

She didn't finish, but head on one side, she looked at him questioningly.

'That would be kind of you,' he replied gruffly. 'But first, Andrew and I must talk. I . . .'

Remembering Edward's long-standing attitude towards Andrew and his work, Victoria withdrew her hand as she said sharply, 'Andrew might not be doing what you had planned for him, but you should be very proud of his tremendous talent.'

'You think highly of him.'

From the intense way Edward was looking at her, Victoria knew he wasn't just talking about Andrew's skill as an artist.

The clock ticked the seconds away as she tried to find the way out of the labyrinth of her thoughts. Then eventually she nodded, not because she had reached a decision, but because in some odd way, what she thought of Andrew might improve his standing in his grandfather's esteem. If she had been astonished at Edward's confession about Alexander, then his next question left her open-mouthed.

'Do you love him? Is that what this meeting here was about?' Then hurriedly he added, 'I've no right asking that. But you see, I've been hoping. Andrew needs a family. You seemed so right for him and he obviously gets on well with Alexander.'

'How did you know about Andrew and Alexander?' Victoria asked. 'There are no such things as secrets around here, are there?' she added.

'Even immersed in my work, the world in the shape of Polly and Mrs Pritchard does get through to me occasionally. When they want me to know something, they either talk very loudly to each other outside my study, or Polly mutters away if I pass her when she's cleaning.'

'Why did you visit us at Ludlow?' Victoria asked. 'Had it something to do with Polly and Mrs Pritchard?'

'Indirectly, I suppose it did. Eventually it did get through to me that Andrew was spending a great deal of time there and when Howard Reece asked me to go and look at some books he thought might interest me . . . I must be getting old, for I had a great desire to meddle in the affairs of others. I don't know why, but I thought if you and your mother saw I wasn't an ogre, it might tip the scales a little more in Andrew's favour.'

'I like Andrew for himself,' Victoria replied stiffly, 'not because of you or because you think he needs a family. He has a family already — his mother and you.'

'I wasn't meaning his mother and me, although after this evening I fully intended to make amends. I was meaning a young family. Victoria, you're far too intelligent not to know what I mean.'

She stared into the fire. Did Edward know Andrew had proposed? But, no, Andrew wouldn't have told him, and even that know-all Polly couldn't have guessed. She didn't know she was smiling until Edward spoke.

'Do I take it my hopes for Andrew haven't fallen on stony ground?'

Slowly she nodded just the once, but dared not speak. She had lost one man through violence. Had she now lost another? Rising stiffly, Edward touched Victoria's bowed shoulders gently.

'Come back to Upper House with me.'

'I'll stay here,' she said, avoiding his searching look.

She heard him walk slowly across the room, heard the front door open and then shut softly, but seconds later she jumped to her feet. The house was too quiet. It was as though it was holding its breath. Like a directionless, clockwork toy she moved swiftly about

193

the room, lifting a vase, picking up a book, straightening the pottery dog on the mantelpiece.

Then she turned to the cluttered table. Scooping up a sheaf of scattered sketches, she looked through them with unseeing eyes, until she found her own face looking up at her. Flicking through the others she found several were of her and also of Alexander. She smiled at the ones of her son, for Andrew had caught the boy's mischief, his enquiring look. But the ones of her, she dared not look at. What would they show? Dropping them down on the table, she went to rouse the fire, but the pictures called to her, arousing her curiosity. How did Andrew see her?

Almost shyly she went back to them, picking them up one by one. She half expected to see stern, hard lines, eyes that warned to keep away. But instead, Andrew had caught a facet of her she thought had died with Philip. There was a softness, a roundness of lines that were of a woman who still had

194

love to offer. She gasped.

When had Andrew seen her like this? Had he perhaps caught her looking at Alexander? No, she knew this wasn't so. A mother's look of love for her son was completely different. She looked like a woman in love with a man, a living man. But this was ridiculous. She was so shocked that she did not hear the door open, did not hear the slow, uneven footsteps. But suddenly every nerve in her body pulsed with vitality.

'Andrew?' she questioned.

She turned. He was so close that she stumbled. He caught her, then hesitated, holding her at arms' length. It seemed as though they looked deep into each other's eyes for an eternity. Andrew's unashamedly showed his deep love, but Victoria's mirrored her turmoil — relief, puzzlement.

That day, Andrew had again seen injured people and the terrible memories this had stirred made him now throw caution to the winds. His grip on her tightened as he pulled her to him. She opened her mouth to protest but he covered it with his eager, demanding lips. She froze and would have pulled away, but Andrew had imprisoned her with his arms and then with his lips. Slowly, like a frightened bird, she stilled. Then as the blood began to pound, awakening her frozen heart, she responded with a passion so sudden that he broke away.

'This is me, Andrew,' he said harshly, 'not Philip. I'm no substitute for any man.'

'I know that now,' she said. 'I can't forget Philip and he lives on in Alexander, but you . . . you are my future.'

They kissed until their hunger had been as satisfied as it could be. Then as he held her close, Andrew whispered, 'Listen? It's stopped raining.'

Her reply was muffled as much by tears as by his closeness.

'The black clouds have parted for both of us,' she whispered. Then

tipping back her head the better to
see him, she whispered, 'I always want
to walk in the sunshine of your love.'

THE END

A SUMMER FOLLY

Peggy Loosemore Jones

Philippa Southcott was a very ambitious musician. When she gave a recital on her harp in the village church she met tall, dark-haired Alex Penfold, who had recently inherited the local Manor House, and couldn't get him out of her mind. Philippa didn't want anything or anyone to interfere with her career, least of all a man as disturbing as Alex, but keeping him at a distance turned out to be no easy matter!

IMPOSSIBLE LOVE

Caroline Joyce

When Maria goes to live with her half-brother on the Isle of Man, she finds employment as a lady's maid to the autocratic Mrs. Pennington. Maria finds herself becoming very attracted to the Penningtons' only son, Daniel, but fights against it as he is from a different class. She becomes engaged to Rob Cregeen, who takes a job in the Penningtons' mines. But when Rob is killed in a mining disaster, Maria blames the Penningtons . . .

THE FLAUNTING MOON

Catherine Darby

Purity Makin is only a girl when James Rodale, a handsome cavalier, seeks shelter at Ladymoon Manor, the house on the moors which holds strange echoes of its sinister past. But the girl has the passions of a woman, and from the events of a night springs a tale of promises betrayed and twisted jealousies; a tale in which a sacred chalice is used for good or evil to satisfy the desires of those who discover the secret of the Moon Goddess.